DEAD WRONG

by

Sylvie Grayson

Dead Wrong is a work of fiction. Names, characters, places and incidents are products of the author's imagination or are used fictitiously. Any resemblance to actual events or locales or persons, living or dead, is entirely coincidental.

Except for use in any review, the reproduction or utilization of this work in whole or in part in any form by any electronic, mechanical or other means, now known or hereafter invented, including xerography, photocopying and recording, or in any information storage or retrieval system, is forbidden without the written permission of the author or publisher.

GREAT WESTERN PUBLISHING c/o
sylviegraysonauthor@gmail.com

Copyright © 2018 by Sylvie Grayson
All rights reserved.

For information contact
sylviegraysonauthor@gmail.com
www.sylviegrayson.com

ISBN: 978-1-7750405-6-9

Great Western Publishing is a registered trademark of Sylvie Grayson.

Cover art by Steven Novak   novakillustration@gmail.com

Other books by Sylvie Grayson

Contemporary romantic suspense

Suspended Animation

The Lies He Told Me

Legal Obstruction

My Best Mistake

Moon Shine

False Confession

Prairie Storm

Praise for Sylvie Grayson's books

I've been reading Sylvie Grayson - can't seem to put them down. How do you come up with these exciting mysteries? Very fun reading!!

Suspended Animation

Wow! This book is amazing, its very well written and the characters are very well developed. This is my first book by Sylvie Grayson and it won't be my last. I was hooked from the first page and this book was very hard to put down.

Interesting characters, family conflicts and divided loyalties make this a book that kept me up half the night

Legal Obstruction

I loved this book! I've found my new favorite author. Emily is a fiercely professional woman who is on her own and determined to protect her little family. Joe is a solitary guy who often doesn't deal with problems until they are front and center. But boy does Emily wake him up and does he take notice. Add in a wildcard assistant and a few unsavory characters and I was up all night finishing the book to find out what happens.

The Lies He Told Me

If you are a fan of the heartwarming craftiness and domesticity of a Debbie McComber romance, and the intense intrigues of Danielle Steele, you'll enjoy the writing style of Sylvie Grayson; where the bad guys are not heartless, and the good guys are virtually flawless.

Just a quick note to let you know how much I enjoyed your book. You drew on your vast experience as a result of being a female, a wife, lover, mother, business woman, lawyer, friend, gardener, homeowner, compassionate and caring individual. It was an intriguing read which kept me guessing and very interested. Well done, Sylvie.

The Last War: Book One, Khandarken Rising

The General of Khandarken sends his son, Dante, to investigate the situation. When Dante meets the lovely Beth, she eyes him with suspicion. But he won't stop until he solves the tangle of motives, fueled by greed, which threaten Beth and her family. I enjoyed this book very much. The well-developed characters and sensuous love scenes make this a page turner. I look forward to reading Book Two and Book Three

… this story is one of a kind in its own and couldn't be truly compared to anything but itself. It has so many unique characteristics to it. The personal relationships are intriguing and different from many other fictional relationships. The names are cool, the plot gets thicker with each page, and I loved the author's style. It became evident that I was addicted to reading the book once I was sad to be finished. I'm going to give this a strong recommendation. It's my kind of book.

The Last War: Book Two, Son of the Emperor

I am a big fan of The Last War series. I loved Book One, the story of Major Dante Regiment and Beth Farmer. The dystopian world Grayson has created, where women are scarce, and Clones are used to replace them, where the Emperor has finally been defeated but his son takes up the fight, just gets better in this second book. …Thrills abound on the race to freedom and home. I really enjoyed this book and can't wait for Book Three. Grayson has great imagination; the fantasy series is awesome.

Truth and Treachery, The Last War: Book Three

Ok, this series is just getting better and better. The increasing complexity of the characters and the development of lead characters is a pleasure to read. The plot, with its twists and turns, intrigue and adventure, is a real joy. If you liked the first two books in The Last War series (and, seriously, that's the place to start before reading this book - it's worth doing) then you will love this book.

Weapon of Tyrants, The Last War: Book Four

The Last War has been a truly excellent series so far, and Weapon of Tyrants is staying strong. Exciting, full of intrigue and adventure, wonderfully developed strong lead characters with a great supporting cast, neat world-building and excellent writing. I mean, what more can you ask for? You do need to start with book 1 in this series, but it too was excellent so you can't go wrong, and I can guarantee you'll have a ball with this one when you reach it.

Prince of Jiran, The Last War: Book Five

I was surprised and completely enthralled! I haven't read a book like this ever. I could not put it down. You fall in love with prince Shandro and princess China Who against all odds fall in love. Their long journey and the difficulties with Judson set this up partner from most other books. This is a book you'll love and have to read from beginning to end without putting it down! Very highly recommended!

DEDICATION

To Mrs. Archer, my Grade Four teacher. She recognized the potential of a very shy and quiet child and helped her blossom.

I am blessed with wonderful support that has enabled me to write. To my husband, who is always ready to listen, read and lend a hand with difficult passages. To my children who had faith in me and helped with their interest, support and practical suggestions.

Any errors or omissions are mine alone.

Sylvie Grayson
www.sylviegrayson.com *or*
sylviegraysonauthor@gmail.com

DEAD
WRONG

Prologue

He drove into the shadows of the old parking lot and drew his battered black pickup to a halt near the building entrance. There were a few cars scattered across the cracked blacktop but no one else was in sight. The apartment building was old, a three-floor walk-up with battered stucco-clad walls and a flat roof. It had clearly seen better days.

The sky was heavily overcast and it looked like rain was imminent. Maybe that's why everyone was indoors on this dreary February evening.

He stepped out of the cab of his truck and stared at the building, hoping Billy was home. It was time to sort out a few things that had been left untended too long. He was in no rush to begin the encounter. On second thought, knowing how Billy operated, he was better safe than sorry. He reached behind the driver's seat to grab the tire iron.

Billy Zach was an unpredictable man. Tonight, he wasn't going to take any chances with how this played out. But he was going to deal with the bastard, one way or the other.

Why had no one stepped up to take control? This situation had gone on far too long. There were lots of people who should have challenged him over the issue of how he treated his girlfriend, but surprisingly no one had. Well, tonight there was a different agenda, and it was going to cost the asshole big time. He'd take care of things now, because it couldn't be left any longer to chance.

As he approached the entrance, the front door opened and his target stepped out. Billy wore his usual worn denims low on his hips, feet stuffed into a pair of laceless runners. A faded green tee shirt showed beneath his heavy wool jacket. Most surprising was the bright red bruise forming in front of his left ear. Perhaps someone else had already tried to sort him out.

A feeling of satisfaction settled in the man's gut. Good timing, that's what it was, remarkable timing to find him here like this.

"What do *you* want?" Billy snarled, glaring angrily as he came down the stairs. "Are you just hanging out here waiting for me? Coward! Couldn't even knock on my door?"

"I'm no coward," he said, determination rising in his chest. "I've come to give you a warning. You'd better take it to heart if you know what's good for you."

"Take it to heart?" Billy put back his head and laughed derisively. "What heart?" He was staring at him now, a strange penetrating gaze that sent an unwelcome shiver down the man's backbone. "I don't have a heart. And no measly warning from you is going to change that."

"Forget it," he said. "I've come to tell you it's going to cost. Pay up or else. You owe me, and you know it. This is your last chance…"

He suddenly lost his words because Billy took a long step forward and hit him square in the face with a closed fist. His head snapped back and he staggered as blood spurted from his nose. Before he could react, Billy took another heavy swing.

At the last minute, he remembered the tire iron in his hand and aimed it squarely at the side of Billy's head. Zach fell, whirling in what seemed like slow motion toward the ground. The back of his skull connected with the concrete step behind him. There was a sharp crack like the sound of a hammer on tile.

Billy Zach lay still.

Chapter One

Then...

Shelley Blake sat silently between her father and mother in the principal's office. Mrs. Archer, her teacher from grade four, was present and sat across from them beside the school principal, Mr. Downs.

She remembered other meetings like this one. There had been that time at the beginning of last year when she was starting grade three. That was the first time she met Mrs. Archer, and she'd liked her immediately. Her teacher the year before had been old and crochety, disapproving of everything and everyone.

But grade three had been okay. Mrs. Archer had paid special attention to her and helped her move ahead in her grade three studies, completing the grade four work as well. Now they were having another conversation about the same thing.

"She's too young," Dad declared stoutly. "School isn't just about advancing quickly in the learning. It's social, too. She'll be right out of her element if you shove her another grade faster."

Mum put her hand on his arm to calm him down. "Have you done this before, Mr. Downs? If so, how did it work out for the student?" Mum had been sick for quite a while and spent a lot of time in bed. Today her curly brown hair had been pinned up at the back in a bun, but her face was pale. She wore her best dress and a mauve wool coat that was usually saved for Sundays. Shelley shifted a little closer to lean against her side and felt her mother's arm close comfortingly around her shoulders.

Mrs. Archer slowly shook her head. "I've not been involved in moving this fast with any student that I've taught, but Mr. Downs seems to have experience..." She hesitated and glanced at her boss.

Downs puffed out his chest. "Yes, well." He blew out a breath that caused his moustache to bristle. "I know of several cases where the student has been moved forward at an accelerated rate. It worked out well for each of them. It also means they can tackle university sooner and get that over with before their cohorts."

"Sure," Dad blustered. "But what happened to their social life? What sports can they play when they're so much younger physically than the rest of the class?"

Downs frowned and glanced sideways at the teacher. "It's my recommendation that we take this step. Shelley can't be left idle while the other students learn the things that she's already mastered."

* * *

Chris Wright stared out the window. The other sixth grade class had a physical education session right now. They were playing soccer in the field at the side of the school, while he

18

was stuck at his desk in the middle of a boring spelling test. Only a month into the new grade and he couldn't wait to get outside. Mr. Hoag called out another word and he wrote *degrade* on the paper in front of him.

The teacher wandered in front of the rows of desks as the spelling test progressed. The blackboard had the day's assignments detailed on it, and the outline of a socials test that would be given later in the day. Down the side wall, student artwork was pinned to the bulletin board. Chris squinted across at the maze he'd drawn using charcoal and pastels. Along the back of the room was a rack of coat hooks, loaded with a jumble of jackets and coats, a line of muddy boots on the floor beneath.

Arrangement, Hoag said and stopped at the windows to turn. Even the glass in the windows had cut-outs taped to it. Chris carefully wrote the word on his paper. That made twenty-nine, only one more to go.

Horrify, said Mr Hoag, just as the sound of heavy footsteps came from the hallway. Someone knocked, then pushed the battered door open.

The principal poked his head in. "Mr. Hoag," he said, "your new students have arrived."

He herded a boy and girl into the room. They stood timidly in front of the blackboard staring back at the curious gazes of the other students. The girl had black hair pulled tightly back in twin braids, and the dark eyes in her small face were guarded. She looked too young for this class.

"Excellent," said Mr Hoag. "That's it for the spelling test, please pass your papers forward." He gathered the sheets at the front of the room and set them on his desk.

"Now children, we have some new people joining us. This is Henry and that's Shelley. Please welcome them."

Hoag clapped his hands and the class joined in. Henry's face went a dull red, but Shelley looked frozen in place. Her gaze darted unhappily off the walls as Mr Hoag brought the applause to a close.

"Henry, I'm going to put you here, and Shelley, your desk will be in front of Chris. Chris, you move back one, please."

He'd been wondering why that extra desk had suddenly appeared a couple of days ago, positioned behind his at the end of the row. Oh, well. He really didn't mind. He was taller than most of the kids and usually got shoved to the back. The further from the front of the class, the better, in his opinion. Hoag was less likely to notice his lack of attention. He liked the school work okay, but as Dad often commented, he was happier running around outside and that soccer game had looked like a great diversion.

Shelley walked to his desk as he hurriedly cleared it off. Grabbing his binders and pencil case from within, he shuffled out of the way.

She sat down. As Chris eased into the desk behind her, he noticed she'd nearly disappeared. She leaned forward to rest her arms on the desktop but could hardly reach. How old was she?

* * *

Shelley bent her head over her notebook, entering the first batch of numbers from the blackboard onto the page. Mum had been too sick this morning to get up before she and Lily left for school. Grams had done her hair for her. Now she felt one of the braids slipping out of its elastic and it wasn't even lunch-hour yet.

She sighed and concentrated harder. These were a bit more difficult than she was used to, but it didn't slow her down. Grade six wasn't that hard after all. She read the first question—circle the prime numbers.

Glancing up as she thought about the answer, she caught Mr Hoag eyeing her guardedly from behind his desk. He seemed to watch her sometimes when she wasn't paying attention. Maybe he didn't like her. Uncertainly, she stared down at the desktop. What had she done wrong?

Dad didn't think she did anything wrong. She got her work done, he said, and she kept quiet. That way the teacher wouldn't resent having her there. But maybe Mr Hoag was different. She glanced up again, but he had gone back to working on the pages in front of him.

So, which numbers were prime numbers? Usually this was pretty easy—she knew one and seven—but there were some larger numbers listed here.

She felt a twitch and realized Chris had picked up the end of one of her pigtails. What was he doing? He didn't tug on it like some of the boys did, just seemed to play with it. The first time it happened, she'd thought he might be doing something nasty, like putting paint or glue on the ends of her hair. But she'd soon learned that wasn't the case.

She relaxed. Chris kind of looked after her. He'd gotten her the cushion. She wiggled now, to get comfortable. It had made a big difference in her ability to do her work, her arms could comfortably reach the desktop. And even though she'd grown half an inch this year, she still needed it.

He'd made Buddy quit teasing her. Buddy had started to make rude noises whenever she put her hand in the air to ask a question, so she'd stopped doing that. But Chris had fixed him. The last time Buddy made an oinking sound at her, she heard Chris whisper, "Wait till lunch time, big boy."

Shelley didn't see what happened at lunch, but when the bell rang and they lined up to enter the classroom after the break, Buddy had a swollen cheek. And as they settled into their seats, she noticed the knuckles on Chris's right hand were red.

He caught her looking at them and clenched his fingers into a fist, giving her a grin before opening his text book and starting to read.

Chapter Two

Then...

School was almost over. there were flowers blooming in pots on the window sill beside Chris now, but most of the artwork on the wall had been taken down. Mr. Hoag's desk was loaded with stacks of paper.

This was the last spelling test of the year. Hoag called another word and Chris wrote *alarmed* on the paper in front of him. He was good at spelling and this stuff was easy. He watched Shelley carefully pen the word across her page. She might be painstaking with her work, but she still beat him with speed. Her hair was in braids as usual, but this time the part was crooked down the back of her head and the braids were lopsided with one of the ribbons missing.

She was just a bit of a thing. Chris first thought they must have put her in the wrong class. But Dad taught here at the school, and he'd explained that Shelley had completed grades three and four last year. Her teacher coached her on the side as the term progressed. The goal was to put her in grade five at the beginning of this year. But it soon became apparent she was too advanced, and after a couple of months they moved her forward into the sixth grade.

His father didn't agree with the action, he thought it was too much of a challenge for a nine-year-old to be in with a group who were all eleven, sometimes twelve, but the principal was adamant, and the decision was made.

Mr Hoag didn't seem thrilled either and tended to ignore her, paying attention to the students who made the most noise. Shelley didn't make any noise. She hardly spoke, seemingly intimidated by the other students. Well, that just made sense. The girls ignored her and the boys teased. She was an easy target.

Yet Chris had noticed, although she didn't talk much, her great dark eyes spoke volumes. The first thing he did was find a cushion from home for her desk and plunk it on the seat. When she saw it, a secret smile curled her mouth and she glanced around as if to see who had put it there. Then she sat down and settled into position. It was obvious it helped. She could rest her arms on the desktop without stretching and suddenly it was easier for her to do her work.

Buddy, the class idiot, had snickered and made a stupid face at her. Chris shot him a hard look. There were benefits to being one of the bigger guys in the class and now and then he took advantage of it. Buddy shut up and went back to work.

But when the cushion went missing upon their return to the classroom after lunch, Chris didn't hold back. He'd grabbed Buddy by the throat and made him cough it up. He'd pulled it hurriedly from inside his desk and handed it back.

Chris had sat down, satisfaction flowing in his gut as he ignored the frown from the teacher. Shelley would have her cushion.

The spelling test finished, Mr. Hoag collected the papers and dismissed his students for the last time. Tomorrow was just a short day—an assembly and handing out the report cards. Chris packed his binders and papers, stuffing everything into his backpack and clearing out his desk. He had a small tussle with his friend Rob as they searched for his missing jacket in the box of lost and found items at the back of the room. He discovered a pair of runners he'd forgotten about, and a sweatshirt he'd given up ever laying eyes on again.

It was a madhouse as the students scrambled to escape out the door, backpacks and bags in hand. Then Robbie went to talk to Mr Hoag and Chris glanced over toward the window.

Shelley was carefully putting her papers into a grocery bag and shoving pens in her pocket. Her gym clothes were stuffed under one arm.

"Bye, Shelley," he called. He knew she probably wouldn't answer, she hadn't said three words to him for most of the year.

She looked up, her great dark eyes shining from her young face. "Bye, Chris," she said and beamed at him. An unfamiliar feeling took hold of his throat as his heart suddenly stuttered in his chest.

Now...

The plane came to a stop in light rain at the Victoria airport and the seatbelt sign blinked off. Chris Wright grabbed his backpack from beneath the seat in front of him and stood. He was in business class, so wouldn't have long to wait, but there was still a sizeable crowd between him and the exit. People grabbed small children, numerous carryon bags, and strollers that had been stowed in the front compartment. Laptop bags bumped against the seats and the other passengers.

He was anxious to get out of here and find a taxi. He hadn't been back home in more than eight months. The dogwoods would be in bloom at the front of his folks' house. They had a bush in the backyard that would be full of flowers right about now. Lord knew what kind of shrub it was, but it was beautiful.

But it was the smell of the soft air—part salt sea, part rainforest—that always let him know he was home. These days, his job was conducted in an arid flat desert, and the dusty, gritty smell of the place was vastly different.

He finally broke free of the push and shove of other passengers and strode across the tarmac into the airport in his heavy boots. Nothing had changed here—coffee stands, restaurants, magazine racks, and rows of seating for the waiting travellers.

Slinging his pack over one shoulder, he headed for the doors. Free at last. He'd just waved to the first taxi in the line-up when he felt a tap on the shoulder.

"What's your hurry, son?" said a gravelly voice.

Chris turned, a grin splitting his face. "Dad, what are you doing here?"

"Come to fetch my boy home," he said.

His father looked good, tanned from all the gardening and outdoor work he did, ropey with muscle beneath his light cotton jacket. His old brown pickup was illegally parked at the curb and they hastily climbed in.

Chris tossed his pack into the back seat and reached for the seatbelt. "How's Mum?"

Ignoring the fast-approaching traffic cop, Dad glanced in the rear-view mirror and pulled onto the road amidst the other traffic. "She's good, anxious to see you. You're not usually gone this long."

Chris nodded. "Yeah, it's been a while. But it was worth it. My last break, I travelled a bit in Europe. You should go, Dad—you and Mum. I know you've been to England, but there's so much more to experience over there. You'll see places you've only ever read about in history books. It's a whole different world. Here everything's new, probably less than a couple of hundred years old, and made of brick or timber. There, you'll walk into a stone church that's twelve hundred years old and soars toward the sky. It'll take your breath away."

Dad settled his truck down to a steady pace, threading his way around the convoluted roundabout suspended above the main road. Then he merged onto the highway, traffic racing past on the left. Tools rattled in the truck bed, and Chris wondered if his father had ever driven any faster. Was it an age thing or had he always taken this long to get anywhere?

"You'll stay home for dinner tonight, son?" Dad said. "She's cooking up a storm."

Chris watched his father's face crease in a familiar grin as he imagined the look of the kitchen in their family home. Both ovens would be going, pots boiling on top of the stove. He'd seen it many times when Mum got involved in the preparation of a special meal.

He laughed out loud. "You bet," he said. "It's what I come home for. Wouldn't miss it for the world."

Chapter Three

Downtown Victoria had been under heavy construction for a few years, and Chris cruised up Fort Street, watching for building numbers. Just east of Blanshard, this was an area with a lot of new development, commercial buildings and apartments lining the sidewalks. Robbie had sent him an email before he left Saudi Arabia that his office had been moved a while ago. Chris was having trouble finding the right place.

Then he hit the brakes. There it was, a new building with an imposing entry and wide double glass doors. There was an overhead awning made of tinted glass, the Transportation Ministry sign positioned on the front of the structure.

Just then, a woman stepped through the swinging doors onto the sidewalk and paused to tuck a cell phone into her maroon-coloured briefcase. She turned and gazed in his direction and his eyes widened.

Was that Shelley Blake? She wasn't very big, but then she never had been. It was the large dark eyes, that she'd finally grown into, and the thick black hair which was up in a sophisticated ponytail, that caught his attention. Yes, by God, he was positive it was her. He took a moment to admire the trim little body clothed in a dark red suit, short enough to give him a fantastic view of her legs, complemented by a pair of trendy high heels.

He glanced madly around but there was nowhere to pull off the street. Someone honked loudly behind him and he took his foot off the brake, easing slowly forward. Still nowhere to park. The guy behind him lost patience and pulled out to roar past, giving him the one-finger salute as he flew by.

By the time Chris parked in a vacant spot on the next block, it was too late. He jogged back to the entrance, looking up and down the street, but she was nowhere to be seen. His excitement flagged with growing disappointment.

Pausing at the reception desk in the lobby, he asked for Rob Bender. The woman searched her computer screen and picked up the phone. "May I say who's calling?" she inquired.

"Chris Wright."

She murmured into the phone for a moment, then hung up. "Please take the elevator to the seventh floor."

Chris tapped his fingers impatiently against his leg. There were two elevators, but only one seemed to be working. It labouriously whined its way down. When the doors opened, he moved back to let the huddle of suits emerge into the lobby, before he stepped inside and pushed *seven* on the panel.

Robbie was waiting for him on the seventh floor when the doors opened. He had hardly changed since sixth grade, although he was taller and a little heavier. Still the same piercing grey eyes and cheeky grin. He grabbed Chris's hand in a tight grip, slapping him on the back. "How are you, you hound? I haven't seen you in ages. Come back to my office."

Rob led him down a wide hallway to a room overlooking the street and pointed him to a chair. His new office was larger than the one Chris had seen on his last visit, perhaps there'd been a promotion to go along with that. Through the windows he could see the old hotel across the street, and hear a jackhammer working on the hole in the ground just up the block. The noise was muffled by the heavy panes of glass. The furniture was new, consisting of a huge desk and attached side table, a bookcase, and a cabinet off in the corner with a refrigerator built in. His friend had definitely moved up in the world.

"I don't have a lot of time," Rob said. "The Minister's looking for information on a new programme and it's fallen to me and one of my cronies here to produce it for him."

Rob fell into his chair and wheeled forward, propping his elbows on the desk, an eager expression on his face. "What are you up to? Did you just get home?"

Chris placed his ankle on the other knee and leaned back. "Flew in yesterday. Spent the evening with the folks. I'll be here for a few weeks yet."

"Yeah, but you didn't show up last time."

Chris grinned. "No. I went walkabout in Europe. France and Italy mostly, although a few days in London to take in some of the sights."

"Huh. Lucky bugger. What have you got planned for this visit?"

"Not much, at least not yet. Listen, do you remember Shelley Blake, from grade six? She was at university the same time we were, but I don't think you had her in any of your political science classes."

Robbie laughed. "Yeah, I remember her. You had your first crush that year. Here we were surrounded by females

29

who were just starting to wear bras, and you fell for the smallest girl."

He felt his face grow warm. "Rob, you're the same animal you were at twelve, and delusional along with it. The thing is, I thought I saw her on my way in. I could have sworn she walked out of the building just as I drove up."

Rob shrugged. "Probably did. We just had a meeting with the Deputy Minister that she attended. She works for us."

Chris goggled. "Seriously? She works in this building?"

"No, not here. Listen, I have to get this report written and filed before they're back in the House for the evening session. Do you want to meet for a cold one after work? I usually go to the pub around the corner on Yates. Say five-thirty?"

"Damn straight." Chris rose and left, a strange feeling of weightlessness hovering in his gut at the idea of finding Shelley again.

Chapter Four

Robbie tapped his beer bottle against the one Chris held and sank back into the brown leather chair, crossing his legs. The pub was dimly lit, most of the tables just filling up with office workers on their way home.

"So, the Deputy Minister walks into the boardroom this morning where we were all waiting," Robbie said, "and slams his briefcase down. Immediately, we all stop talking. He opens up the case, hauls out a huge sheaf of file folders and slugs them onto the table. By now we're sitting at attention and nobody takes their eyes off him. He snaps the elastic bands from the top one and throws himself into his chair at the head of the table."

Chris squirmed and took a sip of his own beer. Robbie liked to talk and this sounded like an entertaining story. But when would he get to the part about Shelley?

His friend took a long swallow of beer. "Now this guy has only been DM of the Ministry for a few months, but we've been treated to this kind of scenario before. He gets frustrated and goes into a huff. He isn't vindictive or anything. Just takes up a lot of space. Wants attention and wants things to get sorted.

"The first thing he does is dress Harry down for not getting his department policy paper out on time, it was a half-day late. The Minister was upset, needed it in the House. Harry takes it in the neck for a bit, and the boss slowly cools down." Robbie finished his beer and set it on the table with a satisfied thud.

Frustrated, Chris took another sip of his own and slid a second bottle toward his friend in an effort to keep him talking.

Rob continued, "Then he snaps out the next file folder and tells Shelley he'll deal with her first."

Chris leaned forward in anticipation, his throat tight, as his friend motored on. "The boss says the rest of what he has to discuss is confidential Ministry business, and she'll have to leave. She takes that with good face, although it was delivered with the force of a Mack truck. Then he tells her the newsletter she produces for the Ministry is okay. That's the word he uses, *okay*. But it's too expensive, and he'd like to keep her on, but it doesn't take very long to produce. She's being overpaid.

"We all turn to look at her. She's sitting there, waiting and staring at the boss. Just staring at him. Because he's not looking at *her*, he's firing salvos while rifling through notes in this huge file and shuffling papers. Finally, he notices she hasn't said anything, and stops to look up.

"Then she smiles. I was sitting there with my mouth open."

Chris's chest swelled with pride, even though he hadn't been there to see it.

Robbie added, "She smiles calmly and says—that's too bad, because the contract is up at the end of the fiscal year, which is next week, and then my price goes up. Remember, we signed an eight-month contract because neither of us was sure how much time it would take to produce each issue, or how much work was involved.

"Well, now we know, she says. By the way, the Minister thinks the newsletter is brilliant. He likes what it does for the image of the Ministry and told me he was very impressed with your interview. She glances around at the others sitting there, then back at the boss. So, the cost goes up April first. And any interviews will be add-ons.

"She pauses to check her notes. If you can't afford it, that's okay, she adds. Don't feel bad. I have three other Ministries lined up to take your place, and the Hospital Board has just sent a bid asking me to work with them. I'll have more than enough to keep me busy.

"The good old boss, he blusters around for a bit, talks about budgetary restraints, tightening of the purse strings, and she just nods each time, not saying a word. Finally, he says, well, have something on my desk by Friday.

"Fine, she says, and stands up. I'll need the contract signed and back to me by the end of next week. I can't keep these other people waiting. She shakes his hand and walks out. I felt like clapping. We all felt like clapping."

Chris shook his head and grinned. That took nerve, Shelley obviously knew what she was doing. Why was he surprised? He waved his hand at the bartender for two more beers and glanced back at Robbie.

"The thing is, how do I get in touch with her?"

Chapter Five

Shelley pulled her little car into the driveway and parked beneath the branches of the Garry oak, just the way the landlady liked it. Anything to keep Leah happy. Her landlady was an old-fashioned hippy, and didn't feel she had to live her life according to anyone else's rules. She made her own decisions. But she also demanded that those around her toe the line regarding her wishes for running the household.

Shelley noted Leah's car wasn't in the carport, but her youngest son's dented red pickup was here. That meant Karim was home.

As she climbed out, dragging her briefcase across the seat toward her, she heard Max give a sharp bark. Her beautiful companion, part German Shepherd, part mongrel, had been fenced in the yard most of the day while she was gone. They could both do with a run. Living out here along a rural road meant she had plenty of places to explore on her daily jogs, with Max at her side.

She slammed her car door. "Hang on, boy," she called, struggling with the latch on the gate. Finally, she dropped her things on the ground, and used two hands to pry the catch free. If only Leah would look after the maintenance on the place. It wasn't as if there weren't enough men around to help. Leah had three sons, although Charlie had recently moved out, leaving Todd and Karim at home with their mother.

Max charged through the gap, his tan and black coat bristling along his neck and back. He didn't jump up—they'd been working on that issue for a few months, so this looked like real progress. But he stopped right in front of her, his nose buried inside the front flaps of her jacket.

Using both hands, she rubbed his head and down his lean muscular back, listening to his whine of pleasure. "There you go, boy. Good dog," she murmured. "Let me get inside." She stepped back and grabbed her purse and briefcase from where they lay on the gravel path.

It had been a strange day, with three meetings lined up one right after the other. It didn't usually work out that way. She tried to keep things in some kind of order—one meeting per day. To deal with three was a real stretch. Maybe not for other people, but definitely for her.

"Come on, Max, let's go inside." Using her key in the spindly lock, she slid the glass door open to her ground floor suite at the back of the house, leaning her shoulder into it. The panel didn't slide easily, usually getting stuck partway open.

The place wasn't big, but it was home and she loved it here. The door opened straight into the living area, with a decent-sized kitchen and island situated behind it. The door at the back gave access to the laundry facilities that she shared with the family upstairs. Off to the right was a bathroom and one large bedroom. Plenty of space for her and in a great spot, not downtown, nothing nearby to distract her, just peace and quiet. And Max. She gave him another pat and put her heavy tote on the couch.

She shrugged her jacket off and hung it in the miniature coat closet, then went into the kitchen, pulling the fridge door open. Good—the power was on today and the contents were cold. One of Leah's boys had been fiddling with the power connections and she'd been without electricity when she got home yesterday. She grabbed a soda and sat on a bar stool at the counter.

Her hands shook as she snapped the can open and took a sip. Then she inhaled a deep breath to steady her nerves, because admit it, she was nervous. It had been a very stressful day with a few issues still hanging unresolved.

Best to get rid of the tension first. She took a couple of long swallows and put the can down. Zipping into the bedroom, she changed out of her business clothes into leggings and runners.

Max was waiting for her at the door when she returned, his leash held gingerly in his mouth. She laughed and gently took it from him to clip it on his collar. He formed at least half her support system and she loved him for it.

When she stepped through the door, she heard footsteps on the path and glanced up as her landlady's youngest son came into view. "Hi, Karim. I thought you were home, saw your truck outside. How's school going?"

Karim was a tall, lean seventeen-year-old with a perpetually happy gleam in his eyes. He grinned. "I heard you drive up," he said. "Figured you'd be going out for a jog."

"Yeah, just getting geared up. So, are you going to pass this year?" she asked with a smile.

He laughed. "School's easy. You know that." His expression dimmed. "I wanted to talk to you about something." He glanced at her runners, then down at Max who was prancing anxiously on the end of the leash. "It wouldn't take long…"

This lad was the youngest of the three brothers. He had taken to Shelley from the start and liked to bend her ear on various topics—usually matters over which he was having a disagreement with his mother.

Shelley took a breath and motioned to two chairs outside in the shade of her small patio. "Have a seat. I don't have long," she warned. "I need a run."

He perked up and loped across to drop into one of the loungers, his long legs ending in big feet clad in a pair of hiking boots extended out in front of him. "It's about Dad."

"Your dad?" she said, startled. "I like your dad. I think he's good to you."

"Yeah, that's the thing. He's mine."

"Of course, he is." Shelley nodded. Karim and his brothers each had a different father. Leah had always been a free spirit, and her three boys had been fathered by three different men. Karim's father had subsequently married and now had two other children but still included him in all the family activities.

"His kids are my half-sisters. And his folks are my only grandparents," he muttered gloomily.

"That's true." Leah's folks had moved to Holland some years ago, and she didn't see them now. Nor did her sons. "But this isn't new information, Karim. What seems to be the problem?"

"Now Mum says he's not my dad. It was someone else. She sabotaged me last night and introduced me to this other guy. Said she'd slept with both of them and she got confused about who was who."

Shelley struggled to hold back a laugh. Karim looked so down, it was hard to imagine what that startling encounter had been like. "There are always tests that can be done," she tentatively offered. "You know that, right? You'd find out for sure who your real father is."

"I don't want a test!" He straightened angrily in the chair, his dark gaze a laser beam pinned to her face. "I've already got a dad. I've got a whole family—sisters, father, grandparents. Why would I want to do some stupid test?" He stared at her belligerently.

She nodded. "I can see your point. And this other man, does he live in town? Where has he been all this time?"

"That's just the thing. He lives in Ottawa, some kind of political job. Don't see why he wants to claim me as his son, anyway. Wouldn't that be bad for his career, or something, to have an unexplained child show up?" He had a derisive expression on his young face.

Shelley put a hand on his shoulder. "Listen, Karim. Why don't you take this really slow? I have to go for my run, you probably have homework. You're in grade twelve, you have homework all the time, right?"

He grinned at her expression. "It won't take me long to get it done."

"That's okay. Put this whole issue on hold. Just because your mum has changed her mind, doesn't mean you have to. Your dad is a good guy, he won't just give you up. You're a part of his life as much as he's a part of yours. Take some time, okay? We can talk again in a few days. Nothing will have changed."

"Yeah." He ran a long-fingered hand through his wavy dark hair. "Thanks, Shelley. I owe you."

She nodded and gave him a saucy smile. "Don't worry. I'll make sure you pay up."

He laughed and turned to lope back down the path.

Shelley grabbed the leash and led Max through the gate, closing it behind her with a sharp click. Leah's life seemed to have always been in turmoil and the boys had paid for that in various ways throughout their young lives. Poor Karim, to have the rug suddenly pulled out from under him this way must have been a real blow.

It was a mild spring day with grey overcast skies, but it looked like the rain would hold off. She started out in a slow jog down the country road, keeping well to the side. There wasn't much traffic here, but always best to be careful. She didn't want anything to happen to Max.

Once she reached her stride, she took the next miles faster. Then they walked. They arrived at the old stone church, and wandered in the ancient graveyard where the beautiful wild trilliums were blooming in clumps along each path and among the leaning headstones.

As she moved, her mind turned to business. With the Transportation Ministry newsletter on the table, she had a second contract signed for the Attorney General's Ministry and a third recently arranged with Finance. There were several more government agencies hovering, ready to bite. If she got too busy, she'd just hire an assistant. Then she could actually take time off if she wanted. On the other hand, Transportation might not sign. She'd just had a head-on collision with their Deputy Minister at the meeting this morning, so she'd wait and see how that rolled out. Butterflies fluttered nervously in her stomach.

As they turned to head home, she pondered all the possibilities. She jogged, then did an easy walk, finally reaching her gate. Max could have done another few miles, but she'd done her limit. Yet she felt much better—the tension had eased and joy slowly returned.

Life was starting to work out for her. After years of chaos, everything was falling into place. She just had to keep her mind on business and not fixate on events from the past. She didn't dare let things get out of control, it was too dangerous. She needed to keep moving forward.

The next Alcoholics Anonymous meeting in her neighbourhood began in an hour. She'd be there.

Chapter Six

Chris jotted down the time Robbie had given him on a napkin from the bar and stuck it in his front jeans pocket as he walked out onto the sidewalk. He needed to get moving. Mum had another big dinner planned tonight—roast chicken with stuffing and mashed potatoes. She did this every time he came home. It was one of his favourite meals, and she went to a lot of effort to get it on the table. There was usually a fancy dessert as well, some kind of berry pie or apple crumble. She was a stellar cook and his job was to show up on time for the event.

Rob had told him Shelley was going to be back at the Ministry of Transportation tomorrow morning to deliver her new contract to the cranky Deputy Minister. Chris intended to be there waiting. How else was he going to spend time with her? He'd done a telephone search, but she wasn't listed, and likely only had a cell phone anyway.

He'd also done an address search, but no luck there either. He only had a month at home. He didn't want to waste two weeks trying to find her contact information.

Rob had said he could get her number from the Ministry files, but it might be more than his job was worth, especially given the Deputy Minster's position on hiring Shelley in the first place. He'd only give that info up if Chris was unsuccessful on his own.

What to wear for the planned encounter? She'd looked pretty classy when she stepped out of the building after her meeting. Maybe he'd better spruce up, as well. A haircut for sure, and get rid of the heavy boots. Time for a quick trip to the men's wear department for a clothing update before he headed home.

* * *

Shelley parked in front of her family home and sat for a moment to gather herself. This was the neighbourhood where she'd grown up, and nothing much had changed in the intervening years. The houses were all standard three-bedroom and basement clapboard homes with decent sized lots spread over a series of dead-end streets. Basketball hoops decorated many of the front yards, and vehicles lined the street on both sides.

The AA meeting had been uplifting. It wasn't always so rewarding to attend them, but tonight someone had told a rather gentle story of having a wonderful evening without even a thought of needing a drink. She smiled to herself. She didn't often think about having a drink either, but her fear was that if she had one, her life would turn to chaos again.

She shook her head to clear it and climbed out of the car. Using her key in the front door lock, she knocked before entering, stepping straight into the living room. Dad was parked in his wheelchair between the couch and a side table, dozing in front of a hockey game on the big TV screen. His denim jeans were loose on him, the knees worn thin. He wore his favourite red and black plaid work shirt. He roused at the sound of the door closing, hoisted himself up with his elbows on the arms of the chair and shot her a grin.

"I wondered if I'd see you tonight," he rasped. He heaved a laboured breath and adjusted the feed on his oxygen tank. "I know how much you love hockey. Didn't think you'd miss the run up to the playoffs this year."

She laughed and leaned to kiss him on the temple, rubbing a hand over the warm wool covering his heavy shoulder. "Wouldn't miss it for the world," she said. "Is Lily home? I didn't see her car outside."

Dad shook his grizzled head. "She fed me dinner, then took off about an hour ago. Said she had some last-minute studying to do with a friend."

"What did you have to eat?" Shelley examined the dishes on the television tray beside his chair. "Looks like salad, at least." The salad, surrounded by gravy and a smudge of mashed potatoes, was the only food still left untouched on the plate.

Dad chuckled. "Yeah, I had a mouthful."

"I doubt it," she murmured. "It's good for you, you know. We're just trying to keep you healthy." Her heart skipped a beat. Dad *wasn't* healthy, his emphysema had been progressing steadily for some time. Too many cigarettes over too many years were now taking their deadly toll.

She glanced away. "Do you want anything to drink? I'm going to get something for myself."

"Sure," he said, his eyes on the screen. "Whatever you're having."

Shelley walked into the kitchen and peered in the fridge. Not much choice, no cans of soda, no milk or juice, not much of anything. She'd have to do a flying trip to the grocery store. Maybe iced tea? As she reached for the ice in the trays, she heard her father yell something at the television screen—hard to tell what that comment had been. She grinned, probably best she hadn't heard it.

She took a second look around. Why was the kitchen such a mess? There was a full day's worth of dirty dishes piled in the sink, cereal boxes still open on the counter from the morning meal.

She wandered down the hall and knocked on Lily's bedroom door. Her sister hadn't answered her phone tonight and with the sight of the disorder in the house, Shelley was getting worried.

She opened the door to find the place in shambles, clothes strewn everywhere, the bed covered with loose papers and open binders. Hmmm. Wonder what brought on that storm?

Her sister's cell phone sat on the bedside table. Shelley paused, then stepped forward and picked it up. Lily never went anywhere without it. She swiped the screen to turn it on, and punched in her code. The sisters didn't have too many secrets and had used the same password on their phones for years. But for once, the code didn't work. Probably entered it in too much of a hurry. She punched it in again but it still didn't work. Wrong code.

Shelley set the phone back on the night table and did a slow rotation of the room. All of a sudden, things had changed. Lily had a new password on her phone. She'd left the phone at home. And her room was a disaster. For a highly organized student entering final exams for her university courses, this didn't look good. Not good at all.

Shelley should know. She'd been there once herself.

Chapter Seven

Chris got to the modern glass-fronted Ministry offices at quarter to ten. He took a seat in the spacious, street-level lobby and waited, keeping an eye on the door. Rob said she was supposed to meet with the Deputy Minster at ten, so even if she'd already arrived, he'd catch her on the way out.

He waited twenty minutes and was starting to get antsy when his phone dinged with a text message. It was Robbie. *The DM signed. She's on her way down.*

He shoved the cell back in his pocket just as the elevator doors opened. Four guys in suits stepped out, blocking his view of the interior of the car. They stood checking cell phones before heading *en masse* for the doorway onto the street. Must be coffee break.

He glanced back in time to see Shelley emerge, then pause in the hall. She wore a tiny green wisp of a dress today with a vee neck outlined in shiny ribbon and the waist tied at the side, the same black heels. He wanted his hands on that waist. She tucked a long envelope into her briefcase and walked into the lobby.

His heart started to beat double-time and he had trouble getting his breath. He'd better not blow this. But how to approach her? She glanced past him toward the door as she fished her cell phone out and checked the screen. Then she grimaced and pressed a button, putting it to her ear as she turned away.

Good, a few seconds to compose himself before he approached. "Yes, Dad," he heard her say. "That's all I know.

She's promised to meet me for lunch, so I'll wait till I see her. Okay? Don't panic."

She shut the gadget down and dropped it back into her briefcase. Chris realized he had to move fast or the opportunity was lost.

"Shelley?" he said. "Shelley Blake?"

Slowly she turned toward him, her expression that of a deer in the headlights. She gazed for a long moment at his face, before she gave a small nod. "Yes, can I help you?"

"It's Chris, Chris Wright. I think I met you in grade school."

She stalled, and he got the impression she was going to pretend she didn't know who he was. But then she glanced down and seemed to pull herself together. "Of course," she said. "How are you?"

He extended his hand, so she switched her briefcase over and shook his hand, dropping it hurriedly.

"It's really good to see you." He gave a grin, hoping to get her to relax. "I don't come to Victoria very often, so it's a real surprise to run into you like this. We were in the same class for Networks 200 at university, remember? I didn't take many of those classes because I was doing engineering. But the prof was great—had lots of interesting ideas."

He was babbling but didn't know how to stop. She still looked like she would take a quick hike if he gave her the chance. "What are you doing here?" He waved at the elevator. "Do you work for the Transport Ministry?"

Her expression changed and she gave a shy smile. "Yes, and no," she said. "I do some contract work for them. Why are you here?" Her smile faded to a suspicious frown.

He grinned again. "Just stopped to visit Robbie, but he was in a meeting."

"Oh," she nodded, relaxing. "I see Robbie now and then."

Yeah, and he'd bet today was one of those times. "Do you? He was my best friend in grade six. Isn't that when we first met?"

Her cheeks went rosy as her mouth turned up in a soft smile. "I guess it was."

He laughed. "You wore pigtails then. Can I take you for coffee? There's a place on this block that's pretty good. I'll tell you all about my travels and why I'm not in town very often."

She hesitated, but as he gestured ahead of her and grabbed the door handle, she allowed herself to be herded onto the sidewalk. She stopped to slide a pair of sunglasses onto that pert nose, even though the sun was hidden by clouds. "Two doors up," he said. "I'm sure you've been there before."

He moved up the walk at her side and halted in front of the coffee shop, grabbing the door just as she reached for it. "I've got it," he said. "It's a man's job."

She gave him an oblique look and preceded him into the place. Well, it *was* a man's job. His father would have had his head if he'd let her open the door when he was standing right there. He'd learned his manners from the best.

The coffee shop was small, and not too crowded. A self-serve counter took up the back wall, with espresso machines and percolators jammed together on the counter. Glass shelves displayed baked goods and salads. The front area was furnished with decorative round tables, two or three chairs positioned around each one.

"Right here. This looks good." He pointed to a small table by the window and pulled out a chair. She gingerly lowered herself onto the seat as he held it for her.

"What would you like? Their coffee is good, I tried it the other day, and there are usually some great muffins."

"Coffee is fine," she said. "No food. I've got a lunch appointment in a couple of hours."

"Great. What do you take in it?" He marched to the counter, a glow of satisfaction in his chest. Step one. Get her to go for coffee. She sure was reluctant, but at least he'd gotten this far.

He returned with two coffees and a large oat bar that he'd broken into pieces on the plate. Not too sweet, might be enough to tempt her into having a bite. He positioned everything on the table and took a seat. "So, have you been here in town ever since university graduation?"

She looked startled, then reached for the coffee cup. Wrapping her hands around it, she gave him a sideways glance. "Pretty well."

"Good. It's nice here, isn't it?" He didn't wait for a reply, just pushed the plate a little closer to her hand. "I left three or four years ago but I get back every few months, so I keep in touch. What do you do for the Ministry of Transport?"

She took a careful sip and set the cup down. "I write a ministry newsletter for them. Comes out once a week and covers any major changes in staffing and programmes."

"Wow." He gave her an admiring look, and watched her cheeks go pink. "Good for you. So, you're on contract and you're using your degree. Communications, wasn't it?"

She nodded and gave a small smile. "How do you remember that?"

"I saw you at university. I think you belonged to the group that produced the campus newspaper."

"Yes." Startled, she looked up at him and laughed in surprise.

Her whole expression changed. That's what he remembered, the careful little girl who guarded her emotions. But when she laughed, he saw beneath that veneer, to all the charm and love hidden there.

His chest tightened, and he grabbed his coffee mug with a fierce grip. That's what he wanted, had always wanted, and he wasn't willing to take no for an answer this time.

Chapter Eight

Chris cut another piece of roast beef and forked it into his mouth. Mum was the best cook, her roast was to die for. He usually filled up on it before he left for the Middle East. There, he ate very different fare during his three-month stint. In most Arab countries, meat was over-cooked and over-spiced compared to what he was used to at home.

The house was a modest brick structure that the folks had inherited from Mum's parents. The dining room was still furnished with the antique table and chairs, a matching cabinet against the side wall full of china that was only used for company. They ate at a spacious kitchen table in a room where, by contrast, everything had been totally modernized, including new stainless-steel appliances and a shiny tan cork floor.

"Dad, do you remember Shelley Blake from school—the girl who skipped a couple of grades?"

Dad paused and raised his brows. "Yes, I remember her. She was in your class in sixth grade."

He nodded. "Yeah, and seventh. Then they moved her to a different school."

Dad speared a piece of asparagus. "What about her?"

"What happened to her after that? You told me she'd been put ahead two grades by then, and you weren't in favour of such rapid advancement."

"No, I wasn't. That's why I told you about her. She was going to be in your class, and she needed some support. I thought you could provide it."

Chris grinned. "Well, I was twelve. Don't know exactly how much support I gave. But I tried to look out for her."

Dad glanced at Mother, then back at him. "I think you did fine. Hoag kept me informed."

"Hoag?" His mouth fell open. "Hoag ignored her all year. It looked like he didn't even know what to do with her."

"Probably true." Dad gave a shrug and dug his fork into the mashed potatoes. "But he was paying attention. We talked about it in the staff room a number of times. He said it had been a stretch for her to adjust to his class, and it would be a real mistake to push her forward any faster than they already had."

Chris pondered that as he slid his empty plate to the side, resting his elbows on the place mat. "Great dinner, Mum. That roast was perfect. If I brought you back with me to camp, I could charge an arm and a leg for your cooking. You should hear the comments about what they feed us over there."

Mum smiled and patted his arm. "I understand they feed you rather well at that camp."

"Huh," Chris grunted. "You've been listening to the propaganda from Harvey's mother." Harvey was a bit older than Chris and had been working for the Arabs much longer. He'd made a career of promoting the work they did in the Middle East.

"Maybe." She gave a secret smile. "At least I'm informed of what's going on, which is more than I hear from you."

Chris felt the heat climb his neck. "I email you," he said resentfully.

"Yes, you do. About once every three or four weeks. At least we know then that you're still alive."

He forced a laugh. "I suppose I could do better than that." He gave her a sideways glance. "How about every week?"

She beamed. "That would be lovely, dear. It would do my heart good to hear from you more often."

His own heart squeezed in his chest. Yeah, he could do that. It wasn't like it took much effort, and if it made Mum feel better about him working out of the country, he'd be okay with that.

He smiled, then turned back to Dad. "So, what happened to Shelley after grade seven?"

"I don't know all the details," Dad said. "I know that after she reached high school, they took grades nine and ten and compressed them together, so she finished another year earlier. Must have been fourteen or fifteen at grad."

Chris grimaced. "That couldn't have been any fun."

* * *

Shelley slid onto a chair in the cafeteria and looked around for her sister. Lily had said to meet here on the university campus for lunch, and she was a few minutes early. The cafeteria was loud, voices echoing off plastic walls and a scuffed tile floor. The food buffet ran along one wall, windows lined a second, with aluminum tables and chairs filling the space in between.

Shelley was nervous, and she shoved the metal bucket of utensils back and forth in the middle of the table with her fingers as she studied the faces around her. Finding the mess in Lily's room had put her in a panic. It was so unlike her sister to leave things in disarray like that. But to not take her phone with her was like a red flag waving in front of her face.

Shelley had had her own troubles at university when her life descended into a frightening kind of chaos before she managed to pull herself together. She should know what out-of-control looked like—she'd been there.

She sensed Lily was in serious trouble, and needed to know what was wrong. Her gaze cleared as she caught sight of her sister threading her way between the tables to reach the spot where she was seated by the window.

Lily grinned. "Hi, sis. Sorry I'm late. My Sociology class went long. That prof can talk, we almost never get out of there on time." Her long black hair was pinned back on one side, her dark eyes serious as she met Shelley's gaze. A rose-coloured tunic fell from her shoulders and black leggings hugged her long shapely legs. Her sable jacket was slung between the handles of her big tote, propped up on a binder.

Shelley smiled and watched her take a seat. "Have you eaten already? Did Grams pack you a lunch?"

Lily laughed. "Nope. She doesn't do that anymore." They chuckled together. Grams had moved into a care home last year, declaring that they could look after themselves and she wouldn't have to work anymore. But she'd said it with a smile in her voice.

Shelley was glad and sad at the same time. Grams had kept them all together when their mother was so ill. After Mum died, she'd carried on as caretaker of the household as if they were her own children. Dad had been devastated at his wife's death, and somehow it just seemed easier for him to keep working, gone during the long weekdays so he didn't have to face the loss of his wife every evening.

"Let's get something to eat," Lily said and hustled toward the food bar. "I'll buy."

"You will not," Shelley said. "I can buy. I'm the one who's working."

Lily snickered. "Always the big sister."

Shelley grabbed a tray and loaded some salad onto her plate, watching what Lily took. But nothing had changed, the same stuff graced both trays—lettuce, sliced beets, grated carrot, some artichokes, endive and a few pieces of poached salmon. They really had grown up together.

Back at the table, Lily shifted her backpack out of the way and took a different chair closer to her sister instead of across from her.

Before she could start, Shelley lifted her hand in warning, "I saw your room last night when I stopped by to see Dad. I've never seen it in such a state, Lily. Tell me what's going on, because I've been worried sick. You even left your cell phone at home."

Lily nodded and lowered her voice. "That was on purpose. No one could trace my movements if I didn't have my phone with me."

"What?" Shelley stared at her in astonishment as her fork dropped to the plate with a clang from nerveless fingers. "Trace your movements? Lily, talk to me."

"I will. Just keep your voice down." Her sister looked around cautiously, then shovelled some lettuce into her mouth.

Shelley picked up her fork again. "I'm listening."

"I have a friend who's a private investigator."

A shudder shook her frame. "A friend?"

"Yeah. He was in one of my classes last year. I think he'd like to be more than a friend, but even so…"

"Okay." She took a careful bite of the pickled beets.

"He's still finishing his degree, but he works for a local investigation company, too. He likes the job, and it pays the bills."

Shelley remained silent.

"He called me yesterday and said he needed to see me."

Shelley stalled. "About what?"

"He didn't say. Just said it was very important to my family, and I should leave my cell phone at home. So, I fed Dad his dinner and drove out to meet him."

"Drove out where? Can he be trusted?" Shelley gave her sister a suspicious look. "Were you alone?"

"Well, with private information, it's important to be alone so no one else hears it."

The sarcasm in Lily's voice cut through the fog in her brain and she gave her sister a sharp glance. "Sorry. Just being careful."

"Yeah, and acting as if I don't have a thought in my head."

Shelley put her hand on her sister's arm. "I'm sorry, Lily. I take it back. I know how smart you are. I'm just worried. I've never seen you leave things in such a mess."

"Well, it's good that I went. But I'm not sure where we go from here, or what we do with the information."

"How so?" Shelley frowned at her salad. "What did he tell you?"

"He said"—Lily lowered her voice and glanced around again—"that the police are reopening the investigation into Billy Zach's disappearance. He said they have new information that is leading them in an entirely different direction, and they want to talk to the members of the Blake family again."

Fear grabbed Shelley by the throat.

Chapter Nine

Then...

Grade nine and twelve years old. This year would likely be the biggest challenge so far, because the other kids would be well into their teens. Just taking the bus for the first time was a big deal for Shelley.

She pinned her hair back and stared at herself in the mirror. She looked like an idiot. Her jumper was new and probably okay for first day, the blouse was one from last year. She wore her favourite dark socks and lace-up oxfords. But the hair didn't work.

Yanking the barrette out, she dragged the brush through her hair again. She wouldn't wear pigtails, like Grams had suggested. It was demeaning. She was too old for that, and the caustic comments from the boys kept her in a state of hyper-anxiety. Mum was too sick to help her with her hair, and she resented that. Other girls had mothers that could do hair and makeup and things that were still mysteries to her.

Her hair wasn't brown or black, but something in between. Typical, there was nothing attractive about her. Although Chris used to say her hair was the colour of molasses. She didn't know if that was a good thing or not. But he was probably just trying to be nice after the way the other boys called her names. She'd left Chris behind at the last school when they transferred her a second time.

Sticking her tongue out at her reflection in the mirror, she tried again, parting her hair to the side this time, and using two barrettes to hold it back. Better. Not great, but a definite improvement over her first try.

She looked closer. Should she get her ears pierced? Most of the girls had already taken that step, but Dad had put up a fuss when she suggested it, so she'd backed off. She didn't even have any earrings so it probably didn't matter anyway.

She had to hurry. If she missed the bus, she'd be late. Dad had already left for work camp and Grams was in the kitchen with a lunch ready for her, even though she was sure the other kids would probably buy food in the cafeteria.

Shelley rushed into Mum's room to say good-bye. Dad had sat them down a few weeks ago to explain that Mother might not get better. She had been sick for years, something about her heart. She spent a lot of time resting in bed. But things had changed, Dad said, and the doctor told him they had done all they could for her. He cried when he told them, which had sent Shelley into convulsions of anxiety. She'd never seen Dad cry.

What did that mean? She didn't know, but it made her mad. Every time she remembered the conversation, her stomach clenched and she thought she might puke.

Mum lay on her side on the bed under a light throw, her eyes closed. Her face was pale, her lips kind of purple.

"Bye, Mum," she whispered softly.

Her mother's eyes opened and Shelley caught the beautiful pale blue of the irises as she rolled to her back and smiled up at her.

"Good-bye, sweetheart, have a good first day. And don't worry, I know you'll do just fine at school." She held out her thin arms, giving a weak hug as Shelley planted a kiss on her wan cheek.

Grabbing her backpack and lunch in the kitchen, Shelley tried not to think about it. Mum would have to be okay, because the family needed her and she would never let them down. Grams had moved in with them a few years ago to help while Dad worked during the week in the logging camps up-island. But they all loved Mum and that would be enough to keep her with them. It just had to be.

She ran for the bus stop on shaky legs.

* * *

Climbing off the yellow school bus, Shelley followed a crowd of kids up the steps and into the wide entry of her new school. A bulletin board in the front hall covered a whole wall. There were long lists of students posted there in alphabetical order, along with information on where to go for home room, and who would be the monitor for that class.

Shelley found her way to her grade nine group and took a seat at the back in one of the battered desks. No point in sitting in front. It just drew the attention of the boys who liked to tease, and the girls who loved to make snide remarks at her expense.

She was thrilled to recognize Molly, hiding in the back corner, nonchalantly pretending to read a paperback as the teacher finally put in an appearance. Molly might be quirky, but she was smart too, and a lot of fun. Heck, no one was quirkier than Shelley, given her age and strange hairdo. Molly had worked on the newspaper at their old school. Maybe, with luck, Shelley would be accepted here too.

The monitor called their names in turn and each student walked up to get their list of classes and room numbers. Shelley was one of the first, with a last name beginning with B, and she kept her head down. No need to attract any more stares than necessary. She grabbed her sheet of paper and turned to walk back through the maze of desks.

Just as she returned to her seat, she spotted a motion from the corner of her eye. Glancing over, she caught Molly giving a low wave in her direction. Her heart warmed as she hurriedly sent a return salute. Not a friend, maybe, but at least someone who acknowledged her. That was a really nice way to start the year.

Her first class was mathematics. It took a few minutes to find her way around the halls and up and down stairs, but she finally arrived at the right room. She found a seat near the door and pulled out her binder. But as the room began to fill, she glanced around anxiously. The class was full of boys, older boys, who swaggered in and thunked their books on the desk or stomped to take a seat and stare disinterestedly into space. These kids seemed even older than most of the students she'd seen in home room.

Then the teacher walked in, young and stern-looking, wearing blue jeans and work boots. He strode to the front of the room and laid a bundle of papers on the desk. Then he stepped forward, braced his feet and folded his arms across a flannel shirt. Narrowing his eyes, he swept the class with his gaze.

"Okay, fellas," he said. "Let's get this straight. This is your last chance at grade ten mathematics. If you don't pass this class, you'll be diverted to applied courses rather than academic. You won't have a choice. Got it?" He looked around with a steely stare. "We're going to cover grade nine and ten in one year. That way you get a refresher for nine and a second chance at ten. Let's begin."

He opened the text book on his desk and began to write an assignment on the board with instructions for completion and marking. When he was finished, he turned back to the students. "Keep in mind," he added. "We'll be finished grade nine by Christmas. And the rest of the year will be spent completing grade ten math."

Shelley looked around the room again. There were three girls here, including herself. Everyone appeared to be sixteen or seventeen, and no one had paid any attention to her. She felt like a mouse hiding in the corner as she copied the assignment from the board.

When the bell rang and the other students stood and charged for the door, she wended her way to the front of the classroom. "Mr. Gaither," she said. "My name's Shelley Blake and I think I'm in the wrong classroom."

"Let's see your sheet," he said, pointing at it in her hand. "Yes, here you are. Right room, right class."

At her determined shake of the head, he frowned and picked up a sheaf of papers from his desk. "Ah, I see. Yes, I was told about you. You're not my typical math student. Most of these kids have failed math once or twice. But even so, the purpose is to combine grades nine and ten and complete them in one year. That's why the principal has enrolled you here. It'll give you a leg up to graduate earlier."

Shelley's heart sank.

Chapter Ten

Now...

Shelley threw the chew toy and Max leaped into the air, missing it by inches. He raced across the yard and clamped his jaw around the heavy rubber, then ran back to her. A solid wooden fence encircled the side yard, giving some privacy for her suite and a place for Max to play. Luckily Leah had a service cut the lawns, or it would have likely been knee-deep in grass.

"Good boy," she said, grabbing the end and tugging lightly as he bit down harder to keep it in his mouth. "Good dog." She laughed as she pulled on it. "You have to let go, so I can throw it again."

As she wrestled the dog for possession of his toy, she heard the low rumble of an engine in her drive. The sound died, then she spotted a familiar face peering over the fence from the direction of the driveway. It was Chris Wright.

"Hi, Shelley. Need some help?" he called. "That dog sure knows how to hang on."

She stared at him. *Why was he here?* It was a very strange coincidence to run into him two days in a row. And she hadn't really run into him this time...

He gave an engaging grin. "I just happened to see your car in the driveway. Want to go for a run? I've been dying to get out and you mentioned you like to have a run every day. Does your dog go with you?"

She had to laugh. He looked so at home, peering over the boards of her fence. Max woofed a few times, then raced over to sniff along the bottom of the gate.

"Yes, I like to run. What are you *doing* here?"

He walked to the gate and opened it without a struggle, which just ticked her off. He was tall, taller than she remembered, and well built. His broad shoulders filled out the black tee-shirt he wore tucked into tight jeans, with a heavy blue cotton shirt slung loosely over it. His tawny hair had a curl to it and was brushed back from his forehead.

"I was driving around the neighbourhood and recognized your car. Is this your apartment?" He gestured at her sliding glass door that stood open to the weak spring sun.

"Yes. I've been here a couple of years."

"Looks great." He smiled again and she couldn't help but return it. "Got time for a jog?"

She looked down at his white and blue runners. "Okay. I could do that."

"Great. I'll keep doggie happy while you get ready."

"His name's Max," she said. "Just throw the toy, he loves it." As she turned to go in, she saw Max had deposited the orange rubber device at her visitor's feet. Then he stood back and waited expectantly, tail wagging, in the hopes that Chris would throw it. *Had her own dog turned traitor? He wouldn't give the toy to her like that.*

By the time she emerged wearing running shoes, Max was panting softly, a blissful look on his face as Chris rubbed the heavy fur down his back.

He glanced up and gave a low whistle. "Nice," he said. "You look very nice."

She glanced at her black leggings and bright pink runners. Shrugging, she held out the dog leash. "He's still growing and can't be trusted to come when I call, or stay by my side when I'm out on the road."

61

"Yeah. That's smart—keep him restrained. He'll live longer." He took the leash and clipped it on Max's harness.

"True." She stopped at the gate and wrestled with the catch.

Chris reached over her shoulder and flicked it open. "I can fix that," he said, giving it a close look. "It just needs an adjustment. The gate has probably sagged a bit since it was installed."

She glanced at him and walked through the gate. *He could fix it?* That would be different, because her landlady Leah couldn't seem to get that done.

"Where do you like to go?" he asked. "I've never gone running around here, although I used to ride these roads a lot on my motorcycle."

She gave him a measuring look. "Yeah, there are a lot of motorbikes out this way."

He laughed. "It's a great road for bikes. The nice curves and straight stretches are perfect for a good ride." His face suddenly turned red and he gazed at her for a moment as if in indecision. "I didn't mean that in a rude way," he muttered. "So…" He turned to the road. "Up or down?"

"This way." She giggled to herself. Once she thought about it, his remark had been subtly sexy.

His face was still red, but he'd broken into a jog and was calling to Max to keep up with him. He was faster than her, but soon moderated his stride to keep them at a steady pace.

They had a good run and she was panting when they slowed to a jog, although he didn't seem to be having any trouble. She showed him her usual route—along the road for a few miles, then up the incline to the reservoir at the top of the hill. The trail took her around the back of the reservoir and down past the ancient stone church and graveyard.

He stopped to admire the trilliums blooming in bunches among the graves and something unfamiliar stirred in her chest. He'd actually noticed those delicate flowers. It both surprised and scared her in equal measure. *What was he doing here anyway?*

They settled to a walk for the last half mile and she puffed to regain her breath as she searched for the right questions to ask. If he was here, she should find out what she could about him, for her own protection if nothing else. "You said you work in Saudi Arabia. How often do you get to come home?"

He grinned. "Not often enough. It's three months out and one month home. While I'm there, I work a six-day week. But it's worth it. For one, I get to build my engineering experience much quicker than staying in Canada. For another, at the end of every twelve-month period, I get an extra month off with pay."

"That sounds exciting. What kind of engineering?" If he was going to keep showing up, she might as well be informed.

He gave her a nod. "I'm a structural engineer, buildings and plants. But I've ended up doing a lot of the chemical work as well, for the drilling and oil wells that I've worked on. I've managed to get a second degree through distance learning while on the job."

"Wow. That's a lot, if you're working six days a week." She would know, having completed a couple of grades at a time herself.

He gave her a piercing look. "It might sound like it. But what else is there to do over there for us foreigners? We're in a camp, all men. There are no women, no bars. No alcohol, other than what's illegal. And with that under-the-counter stuff, there's always the risk of going blind if you drink it."

She gave a gasp and he chuckled at the sound. "You just have to be careful," he said. "It's really unreliable stuff."

"Do you drink?" she asked curiously.

"Yeah, sometimes. Why?" He turned to look at her. "Don't you?"

"No." Her neck was tight.

"What, never?" His eyes widened.

"Never. And I'm not interested in someone who does." She knew as soon as she said it, it was like waving a flag that said she might be interested in him. Except, she kind of was. She had a fondness for what she remembered about him

63

going back to childhood, and he didn't seem to have changed all that much—still offering to help her, sort things out, fix her gate. He was just bigger and stronger, and he'd grown into his good looks. The thought was exciting and terrifying in equal measure.

"I see," he said, and was silent for a moment. "Well, I don't need to drink. If I did, I wouldn't have chosen to work in Arab countries. Listen, what time are you home tomorrow? I'll come by and fix the latch on your gate."

Her pulse calmed, then began to race again. Chris was one of the good guys. And that just scared her silly.

Chapter Eleven

Then...

Shelley stood in the group of grade nine classmates, waiting for the teams to be picked. As usual, she was the last one chosen to join the basketball team. It wasn't surprising. There was no one shorter or less suited for the game. If only she'd get one of those growing spurts that everyone else talked about. For some reason, hers had never arrived. The basketball hoop hung impossibly high against the far wall.

She spent most of the class on the bench, tapping her fingers and waiting for the game to be over. This simply wasn't her best subject.

Mr. Rasmussen blew the whistle just as the bell rang for lunch break. "Off you go," he called. "See you tomorrow morning and come prepared to sweat." He grinned and waved them away, turning just as Shelley walked past. "You," he said. "Come see me in my office after lunch."

"Yes, sir," she said. What was that about? She didn't exactly get into trouble, but the teachers all seemed to want to talk to her privately about how she was doing this year.

Even Dad had lost track of where she was in school. "Is it grade nine or ten, Shelley? I can't keep it straight."

"It's grade ten now, Dad. They said once Christmas was over, most of my classes would be for ten. Although I'm still in grade nine French."

He shook his head in confusion and went in to sit with Mum.

After the lunch break, Shelley went to the office to get directions to the PE teacher's cubicle, which turned out to be right beside the gym. When she got there, Rasmussen was reaming a guy out for not wearing his uniform at the last football game. She waited her turn, wondering if she was in similar trouble.

The student walked out with a thunderous expression, brushing by her on his way. She stepped forward hesitantly in the doorway.

Rasmussen rustled some papers on his desk, then pointed her to a chair. "Have a seat, Shelley. I've got some suggestions for you."

She slid onto the chair still warm from the last student in here. Her math class was next and she didn't want to be late. It was proving to be a heavy load to move onto the next year's mathematics, having only a quick and rudimentary exposure to grade nine maths.

Rasmussen glanced up. "Now, I know you're younger than most of the other kids. And in physical education, that means you aren't as well developed in terms of size, coordination and the like." He measured her with his eyes.

"I can see for instance, that basketball isn't a good fit. Although you did some good footwork in defence this morning." His face had an open, kind expression.

As he nodded his approval, Shelley felt her cheeks go red. She didn't have a clue what the rules were for basketball. Apparently, she'd done something right just by instinct.

Rasmussen leaned forward. "The thing is, some of the other sports won't be a good fit either. Volleyball is usually dominated by the taller players. But, think about this. After Easter, we start field hockey. You're fast and nimble. I can see a good showing for you in that sport. And, I'm planning to start a gymnastics class. What do you think? I've worked something out here."

He shoved a paper across the desk toward her. "If you wanted to take the gymnastics class after school, I could excuse you from the regular phys ed class. You could use the time for a study, or something." He shrugged. "Do labs maybe."

Shelley examined the paper. It had a list of classes and times that would all take place after the regular school day was finished.

"Do you have a part-time job or anything that might interfere with this?" He gave her an inquiring look.

She smiled. "No job. No one is going to hire someone my age for anything but babysitting."

"Yeah." His expression was sympathetic. "I know. It just seems wrong to make you compete with these big kids who've all had their main growth spurts long before this. And my fear is you'll get hurt playing with the older kids. Does this work, do you think?"

She gave him a big smile. "I'd love it," she said. "Can I still catch the bus home after school?"

He grinned back. "Yeah, there's a later bus that most of the older kids take. I admire your determination and spunk. Those are the most important aspects for an athlete, and you've got them in spades."

She left his office with a smile in her heart.

Now...

Chris loaded bait on the fish hooks and lowered them into the water. They were cruising slowly through kelp beds off the Oak Bay harbour just inside Lulu Island. Dad had bought the boat years ago, when Chris was in grade school, and the two of them had spent hours out on the water, crabbing and trolling for fish.

While Dad steered the boat in a slow circle to escape the seaweed, he attached the line to the downrigger clip and began to reel it out. "How deep are we?" he called.

"Three hundred and ten feet."

"Okay." He kept reeling till he was just above three hundred, then started on the second line. "Same depth?"

"Yep, it seems to be falling off a bit."

"Good." With the second pair of hooks set, he leaned against the gunwale and stared at the line of ship traffic making its way down the strait. It was a beautiful day, cool but calm, and they'd already pulled in two decent-sized sockeye salmon. It looked like a successful trip thus far.

Dad set the wheel on lock and came back to examine the fish in the box. "These are mighty fine," he said. "Haven't had this much luck all winter." He smiled at his son.

Chris grinned back. "You should see it out there in the Middle East, Dad. The light is different in the desert. Here it gets hazy with humidity near the water. But there the air is dry like sandpaper. It's exciting, with the wind and drifting sand. I think you'd like it."

"Hmmm." Dad glanced at the depth-sounder and wound the downriggers up a few feet. "I've never seen a real desert."

"You should come, and bring Mum. Make the trip while I'm still there so I can show you around and take you places. I've got Saudi ID so I can get you some entry visas."

"Saudi ID?" He frowned against the sun.

"I work there. As a member of the Saudi Council of Engineers, I get resident status, an identification document called Iquamma ID. It's in my pack, I'll show you when we get home. It gives me the right to obtain entry visas for family. Otherwise it's hard to get admitted to visit Saudi Arabia."

"Sounds interesting."

Chris grinned. "It's exciting. Don't wait too long."

"Why? Are you thinking of leaving that job?" Dad's gaze was keen.

He shrugged. "You never know. There's always a reason to stay. The pay is great. The accommodation is okay. The time off is a real gift, it allows me to travel or do other stuff."

"Yes, but…" Dad raised his eyebrows.

"I've been there nearly four years now. It might be time to find something else that would give me a broader experience."

"Something closer to home?"

His face got hot. Was Dad a mind-reader? "Not sure," he mumbled.

Just then the rod bent sharply and he grabbed it, yanking it off the downrigger clip and beginning to wind the reel with sharp jerks as something plunged and bucked on the end of the line. His father grabbed the other rod and quickly reeled it in before the lines could become tangled.

Twenty-five minutes later, there was another big salmon on the deck, twitching and flapping its tail. Dad grabbed the fish bonker and whacked it a good one. They stood for a moment, breathing heavily and grinning at each other.

"Well done. Mum's going to be thrilled." Dad caught the fish with his fish hook and heaved it into the icebox with the others.

Then he speared Chris with a sharp gaze. "Does this change in direction with your work have anything to do with that young girl, Shelley Blake?"

Chapter Twelve

Then...

High school graduation was coming up, and Shelley was in a panic. "I don't need to go," she stated, her mouth tight.

Dad gave a fierce frown. "Of course you do. It's your grad. Everyone goes. Your mother would have expected you to. Why, when I graduated, my brother Davey was already away from home working, and your mother had agreed to go to the dance, even though she was only..."

He choked up and stopped talking for a minute. Then he took a sip of coffee and swallowed awkwardly.

"I'm not old enough, Dad," she argued. "I'll just look silly standing there all by myself with those bigger kids around me. And I've never been to a dance."

Dad gave a soft thump on the kitchen table with his big fist and peered thoughtfully at her where she sat across from him in front of her empty dinner plate. "Well, it's about time you did. Let's see what we can do about this."

Her heart sank. *Dad was going to fix it?* None of the grade twelves would deign to take her to the dance. She didn't know the younger boys at school, and the idea of going alone to the function tied her stomach in knots.

Half an hour later, he knocked on her bedroom door and pushed it open. Her room was neatness itself, every book on her bookcase arranged by topic, her small desktop cleared of everything but today's work. She lay on the bed, her French language textbook open to the last chapter.

"It's done," he said, a half smile on his face. "You've got a date."

"I do?" She sat up slowly, studying his gleeful expression. "A date? With who?"

"With Leah Cohn's oldest boy." He had the grace to blush. Leah, an acquaintance from Dad's school days, lived on the next street over and had three sons but no husband in sight. "Charlie's in grade ten at that private school he goes to, and said he'd be willing to take you."

Shelley nodded hesitantly. That might work. Charlie was older than her, but small for his age. She'd often thought not having a father in his life had made him timid. But they got along okay on the few occasions they'd been thrown together.

"Okay." She shrugged. "Thanks, Dad. I guess I'd better find a dress to wear."

"Yeah, maybe Leah can help with that, too?" He looked the question at her. "We don't have anyone else around who could do it. Grams is great with the household, but her style is a bit outdated, if you know what I mean."

Shelley giggled and they exchanged a grin.

On prom night, Dad drove them to the high school, dropping them off in front of the open door of the gymnasium. Shelley wore a new formfitting dress, although she was pretty sure she didn't have a form—at least not yet—with a short jacket, that Leah had helped her find the day before. Charlie wore dress pants and a smart jacket that he said had worked for the dances at his high school this year.

A crowd of loud teenagers hovered in the entrance, going in and out through the double doors of the heavily decorated space as deafening music blasted from the stage at the far end of the room.

Charlie hadn't said three words since he arrived at their house earlier, but he gamely climbed from the back seat of

Dad's pickup truck and offered his hand to help her out. His palm was slippery with sweat.

She leaned in the window. "Bye, Dad. We'll see you later."

He grunted and waved. "Have fun and don't come home too late. Call me if you need anything. Charlie's got enough money there for a taxi after the dance."

Charlie nodded soberly and took Shelley's hand. "We might as well go in," he said.

She took a deep breath and held it for a moment.

"Nervous?" he asked.

"Yeah. I've never been to a school dance."

Charlie shrugged. "It's not too bad. I've been to a few at our school. It's part of the curriculum."

He grinned and she smiled back. "You mean you have to go?"

"Yup. No getting out of it." He led her through the crowd. "There'll likely be some punch on a table at the back of the room. We can start there."

"Do you dance?" she said to his back as he led the way through the mob.

"Not so's you'd notice," he replied.

She stifled another giggle, and thought she'd better be careful before she broke out in hysterical laughter.

The evening was awkward, but exciting. Charlie danced with her a couple of times, then stood by her side while the music grew in volume. The lights had been turned way down and flashes of strobe bounced off the ceiling and the ribbons of streamers tacked up everywhere.

One of the boys that she recognized from her grade nine/ten math class emerged from out of the crowd and approached, offering his hand for a dance as the band started a slow song.

"I didn't know if I'd see you here," he said as he led her onto the gymnasium floor, "but I figured you'd be graduating this year, because you're so smart and all. I just wanted to say thank you for the help getting me through math ten."

She smiled up at him in surprise. "I didn't know any more than you did."

"I know." He gazed determinedly toward the far wall above her head. "But you soon figured it out and you helped a whole bunch of us pass. You didn't have to do that." He looked down at her with an enigmatic gaze. "We weren't very friendly, especially at the beginning of the year."

She glanced away. "I'm kind of used to it," she said after a moment. "People aren't always welcoming when they find a shrimp in the classroom with them."

He nodded. "Still, you've grown some."

At the end of the song, Charlie tapped him on the shoulder and took her hand to dance. "He's too old for you," he said. "Even I can see that."

Shelley gave him a sharp look, tired of everyone stepping in to protect her. "He was just being nice."

They left early, but not before she'd figured out how to waltz, with Charlie's help.

Chapter Thirteen

Then...

University at last. But Shelley wasn't ready to leave home. Both sisters were still feeling lonely and slightly abandoned from their mother's death.

So, she took it slow and found that some of the classes on campus could be fun. Molly had encouraged her to get involved with the university newspaper. There was a camaraderie that came with the task of producing articles on campus topics and getting each edition out on time. For the first time, the people Shelley worked with didn't know or care how old she was, or how fast she'd advanced in school.

Living at home also meant they kept the feeling of family alive and vibrant. Molly knew what it had been like. She'd been there in the middle of grade nine when Mum died. It had been so devastating that the only way through for Shelley had been to put her head down and work. Just work. Dad seemed to feel the same way, because once Grams got her arms around the household, he'd gone back to the logging camp with a vengeance.

Lily, at eleven, was the one who seemed most lost when Mum passed away, and Shelley had tried to spend more time with her sister. Instead of getting a part-time job like a lot of the kids around her, she spent her days at home. She was too young to get a job anyway, no one would have hired her.

The girls dove into Christmas that year and decorated the house so extravagantly that Grams started complaining she was never going to get the scotch tape off the walls. Shelley didn't care. Mum had always loved Christmas, and they were going to keep the tradition going.

When Dad came home from camp for the holiday, he nearly fainted in the doorway he was so overwhelmed by the sight. Or so he claimed. They'd jumped into his arms, laughing and crying at the same time. And Grams stopped complaining about the abundance of balls and tinsel stuck to the doors.

Now...

There was a knock at the door, and Shelley looked up from the computer screen where she was seated at the kitchen table. The newsletter for the Attorney General was a new one, and she was still feeling her way with it. Finding the right contacts within the ministry to collect the information she needed was proving to be quite a challenge, but she knew from past experience once that was sorted things would settle down.

Karim peered through the glass, waving to get her attention.

She smiled and walked over to the partially open door, putting her shoulder into it to get it to slide back on the tracks. "Hi, Karim. What's up?"

"Not much. You said we could talk again about things with my dad."

"Okay." She glanced over at her laptop. This newsletter wasn't due until tomorrow, so she had some time. "Come on in."

Karim took a seat across from her and folded his hands on the table top. "What do you think?" he asked.

'What do I think? I thought you were going to consider everything and then we'd talk."

He straightened in indignation. "I already thought about it! I don't need another father."

"I see." She gauged his expression. "Did you tell your mother that?"

"Yeah, but she doesn't listen. I don't know what's wrong with her because I was very clear about it." His mouth was tight, his face like granite.

Shelley tried not to smile. He was one determined young man when he'd made up his mind, she had seen that before. And this was a very serious issue for him. Her heart hurt at his obvious confusion.

She thought a moment. "What about your older brothers? What do they say?"

He shook his head. "Charlie just says I'm lucky to have two fathers vying for my attention, instead of none, like him. I haven't talked to Todd yet, he's still travelling in Kenya and won't be back for about a month. I emailed him but no reply yet."

"All right." She rose to pour herself a glass of water. "What about your dad?"

He looked hesitant. "Which dad?"

"Your own dad, Mr. Samara."

He glanced at his fingers and defensively picked at a thumb nail. "I haven't told him."

"Because…" She motioned with her hand.

He looked up, and she saw stark fear in his dark eyes. "What if he decides he doesn't want to be my dad anymore, now that there's a different one around? What about my Grandma, and my sisters? I could lose everyone." Tears started in his eyes.

He turned his head at the sound of an engine outside, then a door slammed. "That's him now. I'm spending the weekend with the family." His voice shook.

"Karim." She put her hand on his arm as he rose to his feet and felt his muscles jump under her fingers. "Don't worry. He loves you. Even I can see that from the few times I've met him."

He bowed his head a moment, then stood. "Thanks, Shelley. See ya later." He walked stiffly out the door.

Shelley watched anxiously as he disappeared through the gate, then shoved the glass door closed. She had just sat back down to work when another sharp rap sounded on the panel. Max gave a loud bark. Had Karim forgotten something? She glanced up and froze in her chair.

Two men stood outside on the patio stones, one of them in police uniform.

Chapter Fourteen

When Chris came through her gate and knocked at the open door, Shelley was once again seated at the kitchen table. She had her laptop open and papers in piles on each side of the work space. Max scrambled to his feet and wandered to the door, poking his nose through the gap and wagging his tail.

She glanced up, then rose to greet him. Her smile felt strained. She was still recovering from the police visit earlier in the day. "Hi Chris."

"Hi," he said, hefting a big bag under his arm. "I brought some dog food for Max, here."

She looked at the dog for a moment in confusion. "You did?"

"Yeah. I dropped by to see friend who owns a pet store. Got him to donate a bag of kibbles to the cause. He says this is the best food for a dog the size of Max. Something about good kidney function and keeping the joints healthy."

She gave a strangled laugh. "I see." It looked like he'd found another excuse to visit. "Why don't you come in?"

He picked up the bag and hauled it in to set it on the floor by the door. He took up a lot of space, with his big boots and wide shoulders, and she backed up to give him room.

"There you go. Should last about a month," he said.

"Oh, okay." She glanced around the kitchen. "Would you like something to drink? I don't know, some tea or something?" Did he drink tea? Not likely.

He grinned. "Tea would be great. Are you working right now?" He gestured at the papers piled on the table.

"Yes, this newsletter's due tomorrow, so I've got a few hours to go yet."

He looked at his watch. "Okay. I won't stay long." He took a chair and Max, the traitor, immediately shoved his snout under Chris's arm to press his jaw against the muscular thigh. Chris obligingly gave him a rub. "My dad and I just went fishing, up the coast a ways."

"Did you?" She smiled as she put the kettle on and emptied her teapot into the sink. "My father took me a couple of times when I was younger. He didn't have a son to take with him, but I always got seasick. After a while he must have decided it wasn't worth having me barf all over the back deck of his boat."

He laughed, his bright blue eyes alight. "Yeah, I can see where he might think that. I used to get sick too, sometimes, but Dad had all kinds of methods of addressing that issue. It isn't a problem these days."

She set a cup in front of him and brought over milk from the fridge and her sugar bowl. He laced the tea heavily with both, then took a sip. Maybe he did drink tea, after all. She smiled to herself.

"How's the latch on your gate?" he asked.

She nodded in satisfaction. "It works just fine. Thank you. I've been struggling with that thing ever since I moved in here.

He nodded. "Yeah, it can be a pain. Looks like your glass door needs some work, given how you have to lean into it just to get it open."

She glanced at the door. Yes, it probably could do with some repairs. What, he was her handyman now? Confused, she watched him for clues to what he was thinking.

He rubbed his jaw, fingers scraping across the bristles on his chin. "I think I can fix that." He got up and examined it, tugging it back and forth in the track. "Should be pretty straight forward."

Her stomach jumped and a feeling of being cornered hovered in her breast. What was it going to cost her to have all these repairs done?

He glanced up and she caught a smile on his face. "The thing is, we hooked some good fish yesterday," he said. "I wondered if you'd like to come by my folks' house for dinner tomorrow night. Are you free?"

She felt like a deer in the headlights. *Was she free?* Probably. This newsletter would be finished, and she was going to check in on Dad tonight and see how things were going with Lily.

"If tomorrow night doesn't work, the next night will be fine," Chris said, interrupting her thoughts. "You might remember my father from middle school. He taught grade seven and eight."

She remembered a tall, lean, mild-mannered man with sandy hair like his son, who seemed to have lots of patience with the kids. "I knew him from when he did playground duty at lunch time. I didn't have him for class."

Chris nodded. "No, me neither," he said. "School rules about teaching your own children, or something. So, what do you think?"

"Well." She gave him a long look, then nodded her head as pleasure flooded her belly. "Thank you, that would be nice. Tomorrow would be fine."

"Good." He finished his tea in two swallows and gave her a quick grin. "I'll pick you up at six." He gave Max a last pat and stood. "Good luck with the newsletter."

As he disappeared through the door, giving it a hefty tug to close it again, she wondered what was going on. *Was she going out with him?* It didn't really feel like it, and she would probably have said no if he'd asked, anyway. She didn't do men these days. Yet he kept showing up—fixing the gate, bringing dog food. Now dinner with his family?

She wasn't sure what to think, but it felt good. Like someone cared about her. She shook her head. No need to jump to conclusions. And with the cops sniffing around, things could go sideways in a real hurry.

Their visit had thrown her right off stride and left her shaken. When she opened the door, they came in, sat down at her table and began to ask questions. Questions she'd already answered over and over again years ago when Billy first disappeared.

How long had she known him? Less than a year.

How long had they been living together? About four months.

Did she know anyone who might have wanted to harm him? No, no one.

When had she last seen him? That Sunday night when he came home drunk as a skunk and hit her in the face, just before she left for her job at the pharmacy. It had taken a ton of makeup to cover the bruise.

Had she heard from him after that? No, never.

Chapter Fifteen

Then...

This was her last year at university and Shelley had finally graduated from the dorms to a grubby little two-bedroom apartment. Molly pulled in a couple of other girls from the university newspaper to make up the numbers so they could actually afford their own place, two to a bedroom. Dad had been opposed to the move, insisting the dorms were fine. "You're too young to leave home anyway," he declared. "So, staying at the dorms makes more sense."

Shelley ignored him, which is what she did a lot these days. After all, she was nearly grown and could make her own decisions.

Fourth year meant more interesting courses, but more challenging work. The newspaper was still her passion, and Molly hung in as her quirky, sometimes disconnected, companion.

At the start of the new term, she worked up her nerve to go to the homecoming dance for the very first time. She talked one of her other roommates into attending with her. Molly didn't do dances. But Shelley decided it was time.

How would she ever meet any boys, or get a date if she didn't step out there? And she couldn't graduate from university without ever having a date with a boy. All the guys in her classes seemed to take in both her extreme youth and highly visible competence at her studies, and walked a wide berth around her.

The hall had been cleared out with tables shoved to the walls for the dance. The band was playing loudly, the lights turned low, and the room soon filled with most of the nerds and new students, which suited Shelley just fine. The new students were closer to her age anyway, so she wouldn't be as intimidated, and the nerds helped her feel like she fit in with the crowd.

Then a handsome guy stepped up and asked her to dance. He was taller than her, although that wasn't saying much given her short stature, and lean, with his jeans hanging low on his hips. His shaggy blond hair draped across his forehead and he had a shy smile that excited her.

Yes, she'd love to dance. He waltzed with her, his hand tentative on her waist, then took her back to the table where her friend was waiting. "My name's Billy Zach. Can I get you girls a beer?" He grinned engagingly. "I'll be right back. Don't go anywhere."

By the time Shelley and her friend left the dance for home that night, Billy said he was leaving as well. "Have to work in the morning," he said. "The job won't wait. And my afternoon classes keep me pretty busy. Can I give you a call, Shelley?"

She was ecstatic. He was cute and seemed shy in her presence, just like she felt with him. Yet, he asked her out anyway. She floated home on a cloud of euphoria.

That was the last time she saw Billy sober.

Now...

Shelley drove into the yard and parked under the arbutus tree at the side of the driveway just as Leah was leaving. Her landlady pulled to a sudden stop and flung her door open, the engine of her beat-up Volvo station wagon still running.

"Shelley!" Darting across the yard in her long draping purple skirt and red rubber flip-flops, she got to the car just as Shelley stepped out, briefcase in hand.

"I've been meaning to talk to you," Leah called. "Has Karim been down to visit lately?"

She regarded her landlady with a level gaze. "Yes, I've talked to him. Why do you ask?"

Leah shook her head dismissively, her long grey and brown hair flying wildly in the wind. "I just meant, has he talked to you about his real father? He's being singularly bull-headed about this whole thing. I thought if you could have a discussion with him, get him to open his mind to new possibilities…"

"Leah! Come on." Shelley bit her lip in frustration. "He's worried he'll lose his family. I can understand why he's being resistant to the idea of another father."

"Resistant? All he has to do is open himself up to the universe and let events unfold. It's not hard. And it's not *another* father, it's his real father. I made a mistake the first time. but when I ran into this fellow again I began to realize the older Karim gets, the more he's like the second guy— same mannerisms and body language, same build. He's nothing like Samara. Now we have a chance to correct it."

Shelley remained silent, holding her tongue between her teeth before she said something she'd regret.

Leah shrugged. "Okay. Well, if you see him, try to have a word about it and we'll see what happens." Her expression changed and became lively. "Have you met my new man?" She gestured toward her car where a fellow who looked about Charlie's age waited in the passenger seat, working on his cell phone. "He's dreamy, really."

Her gaze suddenly focussed on Shelley's face. "You should try it. No point in living your life like a nun, is there?" She waved and jogged back to her open car door.

Chapter Sixteen

When Chris arrived at six o'clock, Shelley was standing at her door in the middle of a conversation with Karim's father. He was a medium-height compact man, dark-haired, dressed rather formally in suit pants and a long-sleeved dress shirt, although the sleeves were rolled back to expose a large silver watch.

She'd been keeping a lookout for him and spotted the Jaguar just as he dropped his son off at Leah's upstairs. Then she'd darted out to grab his attention and make what was turning out to be an awkward attempt to intervene on Karim's behalf.

"I don't understand, Shelley," he said. "Why would he be worried that I'd suddenly lose interest in being his father? I'd never do that. I've known about him since he was two years old." He squinted in the low light. "Although he did seem nervous on this last visit to our house."

Shelley nodded as she looked up at him and tried to manufacture a plausible answer. But nothing to do with Leah was in the least plausible. "I'm not sure, Mr. Samara, but he seems concerned. Perhaps you could reassure him. You know what life has been like for those boys. The uncertainty growing up must have had some repercussions.'

The man shrugged and glanced around as Chris paused on the path behind him. He turned back, holding out his hand to her. "I'll do my best," he said. "Thanks, Shelley. I don't know what's going on, but I can see your point." He gave a nod to Chris and retreated down the path.

"Chris," she said, taking a step back. "Come in. You're right on time. I'll just get my jacket." She shrugged a coat on and grabbed her purse, then struggled to pull her door closed.

Chris reached past her to give it a shove and waited while she locked it. "I hope you like fish," he began. "I told you we caught a few and Mum loves to cook."

Shelley giggled, then promptly choked up. When was the last time she'd laughed like that? "I love fish," she said. "I'm sure I'll enjoy it."

"Good, I hope so." He held the door of his ancient black truck for her, handed her the seatbelt and slammed the door closed. He got into the driver's side and started the engine. "We don't live that far from here. I grew up in the house the folks still live in, believe it or not. Steady-Eddy type of people."

"That's nice." She glanced at him. "You're lucky."

"Mmm." He nodded. "Probably. When I was young, I used to wish something exciting would happen, but now I'm glad there's nothing I have to worry about with my family."

She grinned. "And you're so old now," she teased.

He laughed and slid her a sideways look. "Very funny."

She was still smiling as he pulled up in front of a house in the Fairfield neighbourhood and climbed out. Suddenly nerves began to vibrate somewhere near her stomach. How would she manage if alcohol was served? Yet, would she be able to handle this new situation without it?

But his parents were very welcoming. She remembered his father from school, and he was the same now—warm, helpful and interested. And no one offered any alcohol.

The fish was delicious. After a lovely dessert the men descended into the basement over much discussion about the right tools to remove and replace the track for her sliding glass door.

Mrs. Wright laughed and turned to her. "Men," she said. "Do you think they do that so they don't have to deal with the dishes?"

Shelley laughed. "I'll help," she said.

"No you won't," Mrs. Wright replied. She was a slightly plump woman who looked very comfortable in her own home. "My husband does them. I cook, he cleans. Come into the living room while I get us some coffee." She waved Shelley to a seat. "You can tell me what you do for a living. Chris said you write newsletters for the government. What in heaven's name would that involve?"

Shelley tried to explain as Mrs. Wright asked a dozen questions. By the time Chris returned with his father, a bundle of tools in his hand, she felt like she had a new friend. It left her shaken—she didn't usually open up so readily to strangers. But Mrs. Wright didn't seem a stranger any longer.

"Ready?" Chris said, glancing into the living room. "Thanks for dinner, Mum. It was great, as always. I'm just going to take Shelley home now."

They left, amid hugs from his parents. She wasn't used to that and felt a little off kilter by the time they got to her place. Would he expect to come in? She wasn't ready for that, either.

But Chris didn't push it. He walked her to her door, took her key and unlocked it. Then he slid the door back and forth a few times, examining the track, and gave her a quick grin. "What time would be good tomorrow? I'll come by and fix it for you. Should be easy."

As she gazed up into his bright blue eyes, her heart did a slow roll in her chest. Now that she realized he was leaving, disappointment hovered where the nerves had been.

Chapter Seventeen

Then...

Shelley stared at the blackboard at the front of the room, but her mind was elsewhere.

"Attention," said the prof. "How do you get their attention to begin with?"

She glanced down at her non-existent notes. Right now, she didn't care how she would attract a prospective client's attention. This Marketing class was boring her to tears. What she really wanted to do was walk out, just feel free for a few hours. Everything was crowding in on her, and the tension was wearing.

Surreptitiously, she glanced around. She no longer sat in the front row of a classroom like a good little girl. She was a grown up now, in fourth year, even if she was still a teenager. She'd seen enough of the world that she could make her own decisions.

Quietly, she gathered her notes together and stuffed them into her over-sized black leather tote. Then she grabbed her jacket from the back of the chair and tiptoed toward the door. No one looked her way or even seemed to notice. Opening the door, she escaped into the hall, breathing a huge sigh of relief.

She was free! She'd never done that before. Always, she'd toed the line. Her job was to get the work done and do it better than the other students. How else to justify being shoved forward in school by leaps and bounds—too young to socialize, too smart to stay in the right grade?

She marched down the hall, her footsteps echoing in the nearly empty corridor. Almost everyone was in class this time of day. Tension was lifting off her like a fog and her shoulders began to release. Then up ahead she spotted Mr. Martell, her professor from Web Design, and she had a sudden moment of panic. She was way behind on her lab reports. She thought of ducking into the washroom to avoid him, but he'd obviously already spotted her.

"Shelley Blake," he said as her approach slowed. "Just the person I hoped to see. Come into my office if you have a minute." He waved at the open doorway, and she slumped in to sit in the chair in front of his desk. He walked around, sat down and stared at a file on his computer screen.

"Glad I caught you. You owe me some lab work," he said, pulling his mouth into a frown as he glanced up at her. "When do you think I might get that?"

She stalled for a moment, trying to come up with a plausible answer. "Uh... the thing is, my dad's really sick. I've been kind of busy looking after him." Her face got hot, which must have told him plainly that she was lying through her teeth. That, and the fact she couldn't look him in the eye.

"I see. Well, I'm sorry about your dad. That's really tough." He tugged at his lower lip as he watched her wiggle uncomfortably in the chair. "Is there anything I can do to help?"

She glanced at him in surprise, and met a pair of very kind brown eyes in a slightly craggy face. "No, probably not," she stammered. "I'll try to get those reports done this weekend."

"That would be great." He slapped his hand on the top of his desk. "Give my best wishes to your father. You know, Shelley, if you're having troubles of any kind, you can always come see me. I'll be happy to listen and help any way I can."

As she left his office, blinking back sudden tears, she wondered how this year had become such a jumbled mess. But Billy would be waiting for her at home and that was never a good thing. She'd better get a move on.

When she put the key into the lock of their apartment door, Billy was already halfway through the case of beer he'd picked up that morning, empty cans strewn on the floor around him. "Where have you been?" he bellowed.

She jumped at the sudden noise. "I had my Marketing class, remember?"

"Yeah, I remember. How could you leave me like that?" His voice faded away to nothing.

"What's wrong?" She stood in the living room surveying the disaster that was their couch. There were empty chip bags crumpled on the cushions, and an overflowing ashtray, a dirty shirt and one sock decorated the coffee table in front of him.

Billy hung his head. "I'm just feeling down. I can't stop thinking about how my mother died. It tears me up." He choked and slumped back against the cushions, his torn tee-shirt gaping at the neck.

Shelley shuffled forward and dropped to her knees, wrapping her arms around him. "I'm sorry, Billy. I know what that's like. I'm so sorry." Her own tears mixed with his as he sobbed into her shoulder.

"Come to bed, Shelley," he said. "I need you."

She hesitated only a moment. Her course work could wait. Billy came first.

Chapter Eighteen

Now...

Shelley jogged up the walkway of her family home. The giant rose camellia bush growing by the front door had burst into bloom since her last visit. Mum had loved those flowers. She blinked at the sight and her steps slowed.

Lily's car was here, so that was good. She'd be able to get an update regarding the PI with all the inside information on the police activity. She knocked on the door and opened it.

Dad sat in his wheelchair in the living room, a mug of coffee on the table at his side. The television was on with a hockey game, the sound turned low, and he was talking on the phone. When he saw her, he cut the conversation short and hung up. His cheeks were red and his breathing laboured.

"Hi there," he said. "What's up?"

"Not much." Shelley glanced around. "Have you had dinner?"

"Yup. Lily's organized meals for me on the days she won't be home. They're pretty good. Not what Mum would have cooked, but still..."

Dad had never gotten over losing his wife. The girls had tried to move on, but Dad quietly mourned the absence of his beloved partner. As the emphysema got worse, he was pretty well house-bound, with even less social contact than usual. The television had become his main companion.

"Lily's home," he said, gesturing toward the hall. "She'll probably want to talk to you." He grabbed the remote and turned the sound up.

Lily was in her bedroom studying, books spread all around her on the bed. Her hair was gathered together in one hand to hold it out of her face as she read the notes in front of her. She looked up when Shelley entered. "Good. I'm glad you came. We have to talk."

"Okay." Shelley took a seat on the only chair in the room.

"The cops were here yesterday," Lily said, twisting around on the blankets, her pyjama bottoms tangling around her legs. "I just happened to be home, because a class was cancelled and I needed to get ready for my labs. Dad let them in and they talked to him in the living room."

Shelley covered her mouth with her fingers. "About Billy?" she asked hesitantly.

"Yeah, of course about Billy."

The sisters stared at each other.

"They asked what he knew," Lily continued. "I crept down the hall to listen, which is the only reason I know anything about it. They seemed to think Dad had seen him the day he died. Dad said he'd met Billy a couple of times when you were moving in with him. He said he hadn't been in favour of you doing that, and so you brought Billy over to introduce him."

Shelly nodded slowly. "That's true. I did, and he certainly wasn't in favour. He made that perfectly clear." Once Dad saw the bruises on her arm, he'd thrown a fit and forbidden her to see Billy. She'd immediately moved in with her boyfriend just to spite Dad and prove to everyone how grown up she really was. "I should have listened," she said, bowing her head in embarrassment.

Lily grabbed her hand and squeezed tightly. "Don't beat yourself up, Shelley. You were really young and Billy was charming when he was sober. Even at my age, I could see that. Anyway, then they said they had a witness that placed someone who looked like Dad at your apartment the night Billy disappeared."

Shelley shook her head. "He wasn't there, not when I left. And how would they come up with a witness after all this time? What did Dad say?" She was almost afraid to hear.

"He laughed." The girls smiled at each other. That was just like Dad. He wasn't easily intimidated.

"And the cops?"

"One told him it wasn't a laughing matter and if he was there, he was the last person to see Billy alive. Dad shook his head and waved them to the door. He said he didn't have any more to say, and they were just talking through their hats anyway."

Shelley tightened her mouth. "That sounds like a challenge to the cops."

"The thing is," Lily continued, "Dad had an asthma attack right after they left. He couldn't catch his breath no matter what he did. I went to call an ambulance, but he yelled at me to give over. He kept saying his oxygen tank was empty, it wasn't working or something. Finally, he used his inhaler a whole bunch and turned up the tank and things calmed down."

She gave Shelley a worried look. "I didn't know what to do. But it looked really serious."

Shelley bit her lip. "I think, next time call an ambulance, no matter what he says. Don't wait. Then call me. You can't be expected to figure out his equipment and whether it's working properly. And that must be hard on his heart. He won't last if he has attacks like that."

"No, and he's been really cranky ever since the police were here. I don't know what that means but he won't talk about it."

Shelley gazed at her younger sister. "I'm sorry, Lily. This is tough for you. I've left most of his care in your hands, and that's not fair. Why don't I look into hiring some in-home care-givers to come every day? We could organize something that takes the load off you, but still lets him live at home. Can you imagine if we suggested he move into assisted living? He'd bring the roof down on our heads."

They both laughed nervously.

"What about your PI friend? Any more information from him?"

Lily shook her head. "I haven't had time to check. Two exams tomorrow. After that's done, I'll give him a call."

Shelley glanced away. The police weren't going to leave them alone, that much was obvious. Did they have new evidence that the Blakes didn't know about? Why didn't they share what they knew? Perhaps she should contact Billy's family. Although they hadn't been at all friendly after their son left, seeming to blame her for his disappearance.

Why was this nightmare coming back to haunt them now? A shudder rolled down her spine.

Chapter Nineteen

Shelley was late for the noon AA meeting, and tried to slip in unnoticed but the leader of the group glanced up and smiled at her. "Welcome, Shelley," she said. "We were just introducing ourselves around the table."

She wasn't uncomfortable in these surroundings. Everyone was made to feel welcome, everyone had a story to tell. She settled into her seat and folded her hands in her lap, glancing around the room. There were more men than women, a whole range of ages and occupations.

Most of the stories were similar. The person would talk about the challenge they'd had that week to stay away from alcohol. Sometimes it was an event they'd attended, where it would just have been easier to handle after a drink or two. Sometimes it was a personal upset that made them think about taking alcohol to ease the discomfort.

Shelley always thanked God she didn't have such episodes. But alcohol had put her life into chaos. If she were to have a drink, would it lead her back into that state? She wasn't about to risk it.

After an hour, the meeting wound to a close. People began to leave to head back to work and the leader waved her over. This woman was a stalwart. Short and square, Penny had chaired the weekly meetings in the basement of this downtown church for the last year that Shelley had attended.

"Just wanted to have a word," the woman said. "Have you got a moment?"

Shelley nodded. "Sure." She pulled up a chair.

"I've been listening to you, Shelley, since you joined our group. And your story is different from the others. Have you noticed?"

Shelley nodded. "Yeah, I'm lucky I don't feel the same urge to drink that some of the others do."

"Yes." Penny nodded thoughtfully. "That's part of it. The thing is, I don't think you're an alcoholic. I think your boyfriend was the alcoholic. His drinking caused a great deal of upheaval in your life and you don't want that repeated. But you weren't the one with the alcohol problem, he was. Perhaps Al-Anon might be a better fit for you."

Shelley stared as her face got hot. Was that true? She felt like an idiot—doing penance for someone else's problems.

"Don't get me wrong," Penny said. "I'm not encouraging you to have a drink, nor am I suggesting you quit coming to the group. Everyone can benefit from a programme like this, including you. I just wanted you to think about it. You may find you can begin to let it go."

* * *

Chris thought he was making progress with Shelley, although it was hard to tell. She was still wary around him, but even that seemed to be relaxing. At the same time, he felt like he was in the middle of some kind of children's nursery rhyme—on Monday he did this, on Tuesday he did that. Yesterday he'd dropped by and fixed the sliding glass door into her apartment. She'd been thrilled by the difference it made, just being able to open it properly. Why her landlord didn't tend to these things, he didn't know, but it was something he could do to help her out.

The apartment seemed small, but there was just her, so perhaps it was large enough. The accommodations in Saudi

Arabia were nicer—spacious private rooms for each worker, and excellent meals provided. But he was tired of it.

It had been great to get the position overseas in the first place. A lot of men competed for the jobs but not everyone was accepted. However, the working conditions were not what they were in Canada and less comfortable than he had hoped or imagined they would be.

The first time he questioned the construction plans for a processing plant, the general manager of the project, a Saudi, had called him into the office and demanded to know what he was doing. "It's not safe," Chris told him. "I don't know who drew those plans, and it probably doesn't matter, but the structure isn't sound. We'd have to do some major re-working of the construction frame before we begin building."

The manager hemmed and hawed, then finally said he would take Chris off the project altogether. That way, he wouldn't be compromised in his other work. Chris had promptly been reassigned to a different jobsite.

Things happened, he understood that. But to walk past safety issues because someone's nose was out of joint was not a comfortable position to be in.

And now that he'd found Shelley, he had a different agenda in mind that didn't involve being out of the country for three months out of every four. He'd never courted a woman before so this was new to him. He'd certainly dated, but meeting a woman in a bar and asking her out was different altogether.

Shelley was different, always had been, and he wanted something more, something better. He was determined, but only time would tell if she would let him in.

Chapter Twenty

"Chris, you're just the guy I need to see." Shelley's dark eyes looked hopefully up at him from her heart-shaped face as she hovered in her doorway. She was dressed in a red scoop-necked tee shirt with a picture of Wonder Woman on the front, and a tight pair of black leggings.

He grinned at the sight and set down the box he was carrying. Max gave a low *woof* and sniffed around his shoes as he patted the animal's back. This was a first, that she openly welcomed his arrival rather than looking hesitant or nervous when he appeared.

Distracted, she gave the box a puzzled look. "What's that?"

"Oil," he said. "For your car. It needs changing."

"It does?" She gazed at him with a worried frown.

He laughed, feeling delight flow through his veins. She lit him up, every time. "Yeah, at least once every year, if not more often. You told me it hadn't been done since you bought the car, so I figured it was definitely time."

"Oh. Okay." She nodded and flashed him a smile. "Thanks." Then she glanced toward the kitchen. "I have another problem."

"I figured," he said, following her through the doorway.

"It's my laptop." She pointed to the kitchen table.

"Yeah? What's the matter? Can I have a look?" He grabbed the corner of the device and turned it to face him. "Hmmm."

"That's what I thought," she said.

He glanced at her and caught a sly smile on her face.

She nodded. "Hmmm. Those were my thoughts exactly."

He grinned and pulled her gently against his side. "Now you're teasing me."

"I know." Her eyes sparkled. "Sorry."

He wanted to kiss her, but this was the first time she'd been relaxed around him so settled for a one-armed hug. Better keep his mind on track. He looked back at the laptop. "Okay. So, what's going on? it looks like it's frozen."

She nodded. "I can't get it to reboot."

Chris pushed some buttons but nothing happened. He turned it over and pried the battery out of the back cavity. "That should do it," he muttered. "If not…"

He tapped the table with his fingertips as he waited, then jammed the battery back in and watched the screen light up. It slowly loaded the operating system. "You know it's old, right? You can tell by how long it's taking to reboot. It's going to quit on you without notice one day very soon, which would really hamstring your work."

She looked doubtful. "I can't get another one right at the moment. First of all, I'm too busy. I've got two newsletters coming out this week. But also, I don't really know what I'm doing when I go to buy one. I have to do the research first."

He looked at her for a moment. "I can help with that. You don't need to do research, just use me."

"Use you?" Tilting her head to the side, she pressed her lips together as she gazed up at him. "That's what I've been doing ever since you took me for coffee that day when we met in the lobby of the Ministry of Transportation."

"Pardon?" He put his hands on his hips and stared at her. "What do you mean?"

"You've been doing stuff for me for weeks. Fix the door, feed the dog. Now you're going to change the oil in my car." She gave him a worried look. "What are you doing, Chris?"

He took a step in her direction as determination solidified in his gut, moving close enough to wrap his arms around her waist. "I'm looking after you. No one's looking after you and I want to be the one to do it."

He placed his lips over hers because he couldn't resist any longer, and she seemed to freeze in his embrace. He kissed her tenderly, his mouth moving with purpose across her cheek to her ear lobe and back again.

Then she kissed him back, and he suddenly lost his focus. She tasted like summer, like fresh berries. His chest was tight and he lifted his head to catch a breath.

Her mouth was soft, her eyes closed. He kissed her again, sinking fast into her power.

Max gave a loud *woof* and there was a sudden knock at the glass door. Chris jerked upright.

Two men stood on the patio stones outside, one dressed in a suit, the other in a police uniform.

Shelley opened her eyes and her face went white.

Chapter Twenty-One

"What do you want?" Shelley was frightened, her fingers shaking where she rested them defensively on the back of a chair.

The plain-clothes officer stepped forward. "Detective Helms, ma'am, and this is Officer Barklam. We've talked to you before."

Out of the corner of her eye, she saw Chris glance toward her in surprise but she did her best to ignore him. He obviously didn't know anything about her, or he wouldn't even be here in her kitchen. "I know who you are. I asked what you want."

"We just have a few more questions." Helms looked at Chris then back to her. "We can wait while your guest leaves if you prefer some privacy for our talk."

Chris stepped forward. "I'm not going anywhere," he said.

She turned to look at him. His full lips were pressed in a tight line, a determined expression on his tanned face. Well, what difference did it make? He'd find out eventually what her life was like. It might as well be now. Then he wouldn't waste any more of his time hanging around her door looking after her.

She gestured to the chairs at the kitchen table and got herself a glass of water before she took a seat. Chris hovered for a moment, then sat in the chair next to hers.

Detective Helms began. "We've talked with your father, Jerry Blake."

"Yes, I know."

The officer raised his brows. "He seems to think he visited Billy Zach the night Billy was last seen in town."

Shelley stared. "He does not think that. He denied it, and said if you didn't come up with more evidence then you're not to bother him again." She narrowed her eyes. "He had an asthma attack after you left that nearly put him in the hospital. That was your fault. You went over there and threatened him."

She felt Chris's hand on her back, rubbing her spine gently. She suddenly realized how reassuring it was to have someone by her side in such a danger-filled moment.

The detective shifted in his chair. "We have a new witness," he said.

"Do you? Why are telling me this now?" She glared, but Chris murmured reassuringly near her ear and she tried to calm down. "What does this witness say?"

Helms glanced at a notebook in his hand. "The witness says a man of your father's height and build was at the apartment block that evening. He was driving a black Ford pickup truck and stopped in the parking lot around six thirty or seven in the evening."

Shelley gripped her hands together on her lap. Dad had driven a black Ford pickup for a long time. He didn't have it now, he'd sold it a couple of years ago. As a matter of fact, he sold it just about the time... She started to shake and tried to prevent her teeth from clicking together.

Helms continued. "The witness said someone from the apartment building came out and there was a loud altercation in the parking lot."

"Why is this witness coming forward now?" Chris asked in a reasonable tone. "It's years since Billy Zach disappeared."

Shelley slowly turned her head. He spoke as if he knew all about the situation. Did he understand she'd been involved with Billy? He didn't look at her, just kept his gaze levelled at the police. "Don't you think it's a little odd that someone with so much detail steps up suddenly?" He waited a moment, then continued when the officer didn't reply. "Kind of hard to give it too much credibility."

Helms ignored that and directed his next question to Shelley. "Who do you think was in the parking lot, Miss Blake?"

Shelley struggled to give a nonchalant shrug. "I have no idea. I was at work at the time."

Helms gave her a level stare and snapped his notebook shut. As the cops departed, Chris watched them disappear through the gate, then slid the door closed. He turned to look at her. "Have they been here before?"

"Yes." Her voice shook. "They came last week."

"Seems strange. New evidence after how many years?"

"F…four," she stuttered. "Nearly four years since Billy disappeared. Are you surprised by all this?"

He gave her a close look and shook his head. "I'm surprised to see the cops here. I'm not surprised Billy Zach disappeared. He was a dangerous man, in my opinion. He didn't seem to have any purpose that was obvious. He didn't work. Hung around the university, but didn't take courses. And he drank non-stop. I never saw him sober. If he was into something illegal, it would explain his sudden disappearance."

"You knew he was my boyfriend?"

He clenched his teeth and a muscle jumped in his jaw. "Yes, I knew that. Not for long, though."

She bowed her head. "No, just long enough to screw up my whole last year at university."

He stepped forward and lifted her chin with tender fingers. "Shelley, no one gets through life unscathed, not even Wonder Woman, here."

She gave a feeble laugh and placed her hand protectively over her breasts.

He smiled. "We're all side-tracked at some point, and have to regroup to get back on our feet. It's part of growing up."

She leaned into his chest and let him wrap those strong arms around her, absorbing the comfort he offered.

Chapter Twenty-Two

Then...

Shelley had worked her usual shift again last night. George and Hannah were so nice to work for. He ran the pharmacy, she ran the cash. They were a good pair. But when the sleeve of Shelley's sweater slipped up, one of them must have seen the marks on her arm. Hannah shot a strange look at her husband. When Shelley glanced down, she knew what it was about. Hannah had seen the bruises.

She wished Billy didn't do that. He didn't mean to hurt her, but the emotions surrounding his mother's death seemed to knock him off stride. Right after she died, his father had kicked him out of the house. Nothing could have hurt him more.

Shelley knew how that felt—to lose your mother to a terrible disease. Having Mum pass away in the middle of high school was the worst thing that had happened to the Blake family.

Billy had been in a foul mood when she'd left for work this afternoon, and she figured it would only be worse by the time she got home. She was right.

He stormed around, threatening that his temper was right on the edge and she'd better not do anything stupid to knock it over. That was always a bad sign and it made her nervous when he said things like that. But the problem tonight was that he was hungry. She got him something to eat and he calmed down. He just needed someone to care for him.

She sat beside him on the couch watching a sports game of one kind or another and pondered when she'd get some rest. Sometimes she was so tired, she couldn't think straight. She was falling further and further behind in her studies, and with the shifts at the pharmacy, and looking after Billy, she wondered if it wouldn't be better to just drop out of university. She couldn't do it all.

But going home to her family wasn't an option, either. She'd finally taken the step of moving out, she couldn't go back again. Grams was still hanging in there, and they'd hired a housekeeper to help her. It was about time. Grams had been looking after them for years.

Dad was even talking about retirement. That was just weird. He'd worked in camp as long as she could remember. What would he do if he stopped? She knew the job was tough on the body, he had a lot of aches and pains. And his breathing wasn't good. She didn't know what that meant but she wished he'd see a doctor about it. When she suggested it, he just grunted and changed the subject. Stubborn as a mule!!!

Now why was she crying? She had lots of things to be grateful for. She didn't need to cry because Dad might retire. She turned her head so Billy didn't see.

Now...

"Dad, I'm here."

Shelley carried the bags of Indian takeout into the kitchen and placed them on the counter. She heard a thump, and then Dad's chair rolled down the hall. She peered around the corner. He was wearing a nice new golf shirt with his phone stuffed into the breast pocket. His pants were pressed, no jeans tonight.

"What's going on?" she said. "You're all dressed up."

106

He grinned and adjusted the oxygen tube. "Lily told me you're bringing your boyfriend over. I wanted to impress him with my sartorial splendour."

She laughed and her cheeks got hot. "He's not my boyfriend. But he is a friend. I knew him at university."

"Yeah, you knew him in grade school, too." He rolled across the floor and opened a drawer to pull out a handful of cutlery.

Shelley stared at his broad back. "How do you know that?"

"Chris Wright. You talked about him." Dad wheeled around and gave her a look. "You can't fool me, girl. You told me he sat behind you and played with your braids."

The doorbell sounded and Shelley hovered nervously, her face red. "You won't say stuff like that while he's here, will you?"

"Shelley, go on. I'll be good, I promise. Get the door."

Lily appeared from down the hall, her usual tight black jeans replaced by a nice skirt and blouse. She began to take plates from the cupboard as Shelley hurried to the front door.

Chris waited patiently on the step, a bag in his hand. He gave her a swift onceover, taking in her ice-blue tunic and black tights, and a grin split his face. "You look great," he said, stepping through the doorway. "Nice outfit."

She gave a nervous smile and accepted the bag from his hand. It felt like a bottle of wine, and her heart took a dive. Lily was the one who had persuaded her to invite Chris to their Sunday night dinner. Now she wasn't sure it had been such a good idea. But when she pulled the paper off, she saw it was a bottle of sparkling fruit juice. She beamed at him. "Thank you, this is very nice."

He smiled, then looked past her as Dad's wheelchair approached, Lily right behind it. Shelley waved vaguely at her family. "Chris, this is my father, Jerry Blake. And this is Lily, my sister."

Chris gave Dad's hand a firm shake, and when he took Lily's hand, her sister's face went red. She smiled to herself.

Lily might talk about guys a lot, but she'd bet she'd never had a steady boyfriend.

Introductions out of the way, Shelley led everyone back to the small dining room. "No one did any cooking," she said, giving Chris a humourous glance. "Not like at your folks' place. We're having curry tonight."

"I love curry," he said. "Eat a lot of it in Arab countries."

Dad nodded at him. "I used to work for an East Indian family in the bush in my early days," he said. "We often had their food in camp. Damn good taste."

Chris grinned and took his seat. "Do you guys do this every Sunday?"

"Not always," said Lily. "Sometimes we get too busy. I've just finished final exams. But we're making more of an effort to do it each week." She shot a glance at Shelley, who concentrated on passing the dishes around. With things so up in the air and the police digging around the disappearance of Billy, it just felt right to pull together.

"What are you taking at university?" Chris asked.

Lily reeled off the courses she'd completed this term, and a lively discussion ensued about what she might enrol in next year. Shelley watched Chris's face. He was interested in what her sister was saying, adding his comments about which courses were most useful versus those that were more interesting. "But what's your major?" he asked.

Lily talked about her goals of working in communications like her big sister. Shelley felt a little glow of pride in her chest at the thought that Lily wanted to follow in her footsteps.

When there was a pause, Dad said, "Are you glad you went to university, Chris? I never had the chance, and didn't really see the point until Shelley decided to go."

Chris nodded. "I can understand that. Shelley tells me you were a logger, worked in the bush."

"That's right." Dad wheezed and adjusted his oxygen tank. "All my working life."

"So, there was probably no need for university, right?" He glanced at Dad as he took a bite from his plate. "You had a good working career without that kind of education. But I bet you didn't become a logger just by picking up a chainsaw."

Dad gave a hoarse laugh, shaking his head. "Not on your life. I started out as a swamper, then on the donkey engine. By the time I worked my way up to bucker, I'd been in the bush quite a few years. I was a faller in the last years. I worked with the best of them." He got a melancholy look on his face.

"It must have been as much training as apprenticeship," said Chris. "That's kind of what it's been like for me. I got the university degree but still had to do an internship to get my professional status before I could practise. They've just gone about it in a more formal way than they used to. Is that good or bad?" He shot Dad a humourous look.

Her father talked more than he had in a long time. Then he pulled Chris into the living room after dinner while she and Lily cleared the table. From what she could hear, their conversation ranged from travel to jobs and a few things in between. Dad delighted in telling about the logging camps, how they worked, the long hours, the horrific injuries.

"Dad likes him," Lily whispered as she wiped the table with a wet cloth. "He's a nice guy."

Shelley glanced at her. "I know he's a nice guy. So, what's he doing with me?"

"You mean because you don't deserve a nice man?" Lily gave her a sharp glance. "Or because you don't date? And why is that? Not all men are like Billy Zach, you know. Some of them are really nice. And good in bed, too."

"Lily!"

Her sister laughed. "Don't tell me you haven't thought of it, because I won't believe you. Chris is handsome, look at the shoulders on him."

"I know." She peeked into the living room. "But with this missing person's thing going on, he's bound to be scared off. I don't want to get involved with someone just to be abandoned again when things get difficult."

Lily thought for a minute. "He's a different kind of man. Maybe he's not the type to disappear. What if he stays? That's the question you have to deal with."

The thought of losing him had become more and more disturbing. But how would she handle it if he did stay?

Chapter Twenty-Three

Then...

Shelley lay in bed and listened to Billy move about the kitchen. Finally, she heard the apartment door slam behind him as he left. There was silence. She rolled slowly to her side.

Last night was so horrible, she could hardly think about it. She'd gone with Billy to a nightclub in town. There was a decent band playing and she was excited by the prospect of dancing. The place was packed. She'd dressed in her favourite top, with the little straps.

They had ordered drinks and then she went to the washroom, leaving Billy with a couple of the guys that he sometimes hung out with. Shelley didn't know them, and had no interest in finding out who they were or what they did. One of them always made her very uncomfortable, the way he raked her body with his gaze. It gave her the creeps. She suspected they did drugs with her boyfriend and she didn't want any part of it.

When she got back to the table, Billy was suddenly in a foul mood. "Where have you been," he kept saying, which was odd because she'd told him she was going to the washroom.

"I want to dance," she said, leaning forward to speak near his ear. He turned around and hit her in the face with the back of his hand. She was so surprised she couldn't think for a moment, just staggered backward from the impact.

Then Billy got to his feet. She thought he was going to take her arm to help her stand straight because she was still wobbly from the blow. Instead he punched her square in the chest.

She fell to the dingy floor, struggling for breath. She wasn't sure what happened after that. There was a lot of pushing and shoving as guys' boots tromped on the floor. Then someone dragged her out of the way toward the wall, removing her from the mêlée on the club floor.

Lily was crouching beside her, staring into her face. What was her sister doing there, anyway? She was too young to be in a nightclub. Lily kept asking if she was all right. But obviously she wasn't, she couldn't catch her breath.

Shelley rolled on the pillow and lifted her hand to press her fingers to her chest. Her breastbone was sore and tender to the touch.

Lily had better not talk about what happened, because Dad would have a fit if he knew. Shelley had told her not to tell, but had no confidence that she'd keep it a secret.

Now...

Shelley packed her briefcase and dropped her cell phone in one of the pockets. "Is that all?" she inquired politely.

The secretary nodded as she gathered papers in a stack and tapped them together on her desk. "It looks complete to me," she said. "I'll pass it through to him, and if there are any problems I'll send you an email."

"Fine. Thanks for your time." She walked into the hall and headed for the elevator, her head stuffed with details. Why couldn't the secretary just email the changes to her in the first place, instead of issuing a summons to come down to the office to meet in person? Wouldn't it be more efficient for everyone? That's what her other clients did.

Oh, well. She was glad to have the work, and the Deputy Minister of Transport was finding less and less to complain about each time. She'd take that as a sign of progress.

Chris waited for her in the lobby of the building, talking to his friend Rob. As she walked up, Rob said goodbye, waved to her and left by the front door. Chris turned, a slow smile forming on his handsome face.

Something stirred in her chest, a feeling of anticipation, or longing.

"There you are," he said. "How did it go?"

"It's getting better. I'm hoping there'll come a day when they just call me with the changes."

He laughed, and the openness of his expression was so attractive she had to glance away. She was in too much of a mess right now to consider getting involved with anyone, let alone a man who left town for three months at a time. Yet, she smiled when he did because he delighted her on a very basic level.

He took her arm and directed her toward the door. "You promised to have lunch with me. Where would you like to go?"

"I don't mind," she said, reaching for her sunglasses and sliding them on. "Any place close."

He pulled in his chin. "This is a major event. You've agreed to go out with me. It should be somewhere special. How about the Empress Hotel?"

She gave a startled laugh. "No, too expensive and formal. Do you like Japanese? Let's go to the Penthouse on the Harbour, the sushi is great."

He nodded as his eyes widened. "You eat sushi? I love the stuff, but I can't get my folks to even try it. *Raw fish?* Mum shrieks. *Who eats raw fish?*"

She smirked at him impishly. "Yet she likes it cooked."

He grinned. "Oh yeah, lots of that."

They were soon seated at a table by the window in the fourth-floor restaurant with a beautiful view of the downtown docks. As the waiter brought menus, the Coho car ferry to Port Angeles in Washington State began to leave the terminal. It backed slowly out of the slip, then turned in a half circle to motor toward the mouth of the harbour. It gave a low two-toned toot from its horn and glided out of sight.

"It's a beautiful city," Chris remarked as he gazed out over the water. "The downtown is small but covers all the bases and the architecture is stunning. Look at the Empress Hotel and the Legislature buildings with all the gardens around them. Pretty impressive."

He turned to her. 'Dad says when he was a kid, the provincial museum was in the basement of the Legislature. That's before they built the new museum and bell tower across the street."

"Oh," she said. "I didn't know that. In the basement? I've gone on tours through that building but didn't know there was a lower floor."

"Yeah, it's probably got a foot of water in it now, just like the Empress."

She laughed. "Is that the structural engineer talking?"

"Well, it makes sense." He gave her a smug look. "They filled in a slough and built on top of the fill. What did they expect would happen?"

Shelley was still laughing when their food arrived—trays of sushi and sashimi accompanied by bowls of rice noodle salad and a platter of prawn and vegetable tempura. She'd laughed more in the last few weeks than she had in a very long time, even with the threat of police action hanging heavily over her head. Chris had an amazing effect on her. And it wasn't just fun, it was attraction. Lily was right, she was fascinated by the man.

What should she do? Her sister would tell her to step out and enjoy herself.

Her hands were damp with perspiration as she grabbed a piece of sushi with a pair of chop sticks and dipped it in the tiny bowl of soy sauce. She popped it in her mouth just as Chris laid his chop sticks down.

"You know I leave to go back to work in a couple of weeks," he said. His expression had become serious.

Her heart flipped over. "Yes, is it only two weeks?"

"Yeah." He took her hand and rubbed his thumb over the backs of her fingers causing a tingle to run up her arm. "I'm really attracted to you, Shelley. I want to get to know you. I want us to spend some time together."

She gave a hesitant nod. "But only two weeks," she said again.

"I promise to come back." He smiled and kissed her hand as the tingle got stronger.

She gazed sightlessly at the sunomono salad on the table in front of her. She didn't want him to spend time with her, then up and leave town. It wasn't fair. She suddenly realized she was already involved. The fact she was sorrowful he would soon go told her that. Maybe Lily was right. Why let Chris leave without having experienced everything she wanted from him?

She glanced sideways and watched those big hands as he grabbed a piece of tempura with the chop sticks and dipped it in sauce. What would those hands feel like on her skin, touching her? It had been a long time, and her body was waking up in a very real way. Heat flooded her belly and spread lower.

She took a deep breath and turned toward him. "I have to finish another project this afternoon," she said. "But I'm free this evening. Would you like to come to dinner at my place?"

His eyes lit up and she suddenly froze. Was this a mistake? She hadn't exactly taken the time to think it through.

Chapter Twenty-Four

Then...

Shelley finished up her shift at work and hung up her smock in the staff room. Then she climbed into her car to head home, knowing things were still rocky with Billy. He'd already started drinking by the time she left for the pharmacy this afternoon. He'd bought the usual case of beer and there were six empties scattered on the coffee table as she took her purse and left the apartment. She dreaded what condition he'd be in upon her return.

She parked in the lot outside the building and noted Billy's Jeep in its usual spot. She glanced up at their window. The lights were on. Tiptoeing into the apartment, she closed the door quietly behind her in the hopes he was already asleep.

The TV was on the history channel. Strange, he didn't usually watch that. There were beer cans all over the place and empty chip bags on the couch. Hopefully, he was in bed asleep because otherwise there would be another huge row. He hated being left alone, and a case of beer always resulted in a vicious argument.

She undressed silently in the bathroom, turning all the lights off as she went. But when she crept quietly into bed and felt across the mattress, it was empty. She flicked on the light. No Billy.

Shelley flopped onto her back in relief. He'd gone out, that was the best possible result. No fight tonight.

When she woke in the morning after a good night's sleep, she was still alone in the apartment. It wasn't the first time he'd done this, but she was grateful nonetheless. Not to have to deal with a drunken Billy was a gift.

She was tired. Lying in bed, she ran through the juggling act that was her life—dealing with Billy, handling a full course load, falling behind in her classwork, working part-time at the pharmacy. It was almost more than she could handle.

She sighed and sat up. At least this morning she was free to get ready and head to class without an argument of any kind. Given that the term was almost over, maybe she could even rescue a few of those courses she was taking—get the work completed and handed in, even if it was late, just to get a passing grade. Of all her profs, Mr. Martell was the most patient. She could probably get enough labs done to complete the Web Design course.

She'd skipped so many classes now, she knew a lot of her profs wouldn't give her the time of day. But there was always a chance.

As she pulled the apartment door closed behind her and listened for the lock to click, she wondered where Billy was. He was going to be in a foul mood when he got home. He always was.

* * *

It had been three long days since she'd last seen Billy. He had simply disappeared, leaving everything behind. His clothes were still in the closet, the mess of papers, screws and pens on the night table at his side of the bed. He'd even left his Jeep with the camouflage paint, still sitting in the parking lot at the side of the building. Shelley tried calling him, but he didn't answer his phone, every call going straight to voice mail. Nor had he called her, no matter how many messages she left.

The day after he disappeared, she'd found a note on a pad of paper on the coffee table in the living room. *Leave me alone!* No signature, but it looked like Billy's handwriting and who else would have put it there?

She was stunned. Why would he abandon her like this? Had he found someone else to hook up with, or simply taken off travelling again? He'd talked so often about doing another trip to Europe. The first time he'd been gone a year, he said. What would it be like this time?

Above all, why didn't he talk to her about his plans? She was in a rage, and at the same time, totally humiliated. Her biggest fear was he'd gone off on a bender. If so, he was going to be in a really foul mood when he got back.

Shelley rolled in the bedclothes, trying to talk herself into driving up to the university to attend a class, any class. When the doorbell shrilled, she startled. Who would be out there this time of the morning? Maybe Billy lost his key!

She leapt from the bed and grabbed her housecoat from the back of the bathroom door.

It wasn't Billy. It was his father, and a woman she'd never seen before.

"What do you want?" She glared at Mr Zach, who stood uneasily on the front step. "Billy isn't here."

"I know he's not here," he growled. "He borrowed some things from me and I want them back."

Her gaze skittered to the woman behind him. "Who are you?" she blurted. It wasn't like her to be so rude, but something had broken inside at being abandoned like this.

Zach gestured at the woman as he walked past into the hall. "Billy's mother."

Shelley took a feeble step back in shock as they barged past. *His mother? His mother was dead!* He'd told her many times his mother had died. The realization it had been a lie was like a knife in her chest.

She staggered into the kitchen to find Mrs. Zach rifling through the fridge for something to eat. In a daze, Shelley watched her. What were they doing? Obviously, they'd heard from their son, because they already knew he wouldn't be here.

Sidling around the heavy woman, she flicked the kettle on and spooned instant coffee into a mug. "Do you know where Billy is?" she asked, her voice coming out thin and shrill.

His mother glanced at her and raised her brows, then dove back into the fridge.

"Has he gone back to Europe?" She was suddenly nauseous and swallowed hard to contain the surge of bile in her throat.

"Back to Europe? He's never been to Europe." Mrs. Zach's mouth was stretched in a thin smile.

Shelley poured hot water into her mug with an unsteady hand. "He spent a year there, he told me," she said.

His mother laughed derisively. "He spent a year in jail."

She stared at the woman's broad back as she turned to the cupboards, opening them one at a time. *Billy had been in jail? When? What for?* Her world wobbled on its axis. Then she heard rustling in the bedroom and hurried into the hall to peer through the doorway.

Mr. Zach was combing the closet, tearing Billy's clothes from the hangers and stuffing them into plastic bags. He moved to the dresser and began emptying drawers onto the bed. Where did he get all the bags? Must have brought them with him.

"What are you doing?" she shrieked.

He ignored her and bent to pull an old backpack from under her night table. "Whose is this?" he asked.

"That's mine." Shelley had used it for college the first few years she'd attended.

He unzipped the pockets and fished around inside.

"I said, that's mine!" She grabbed for it and he smiled, holding it above his head out of her reach.

"I'm just checking," he said. "Don't know what you might be hiding in there."

"That's it." She stormed into the kitchen and grabbed the phone. "I'm calling the police."

119

"Hey." Mr. Zach appeared behind her. "That won't be necessary." He seized the phone out of her hand and hung it up in the cradle as she subsided onto the couch cushions in defeat.

He gave a short nod to his wife, and as Mrs. Zach gathered together the food she'd pulled out of the cupboards, he darted back into the bedroom. When he reappeared, he was loaded with garbage bags, heading for the front door, Mrs. Zach in his wake. He snatched Billy's keys to the Jeep from the counter as he marched by. And then they were gone.

Shelley sat on the couch, winded from the encounter. It was too much to take in at once. Billy's mother wasn't dead, she was very much alive. His father didn't act like the successful well-heeled salesman that Billy had described. Just another lie, apparently. And they'd come through uninvited and swept the place clean of Billy's possessions.

A wave of rage roared through her. With sudden energy, she marched into the bathroom and gathered everything off his shelf above the sink, tossing it straight into the waste basket. Then she stood over the sink, head hanging, bracing her weight with her arms. She felt sick.

Billy must have left town for some reason. Maybe the police were after him and he'd sent his folks to get his stuff because he couldn't come back himself. She didn't even miss him that much. It was just the shock, that he would treat her this way—leaving without a word.

And he'd never been to Europe. He'd spent that year in jail. His mother had laughed when she told her. Shelley didn't know what crime he might have committed to get a sentence that long, but it had to be something serious.

She stumbled into the bedroom, climbed into bed and pulled the pillow over her head. No class again today.

Chapter Twenty-Five

Then...

When the doorbell rang again the next morning, Shelley thought of pretending she wasn't home. She'd already faced down the whole family last night. Grams, Dad and Lily had descended on her like a plague of locusts, eating up all the oxygen in the place. Grams demanded she come back home. Lily supported her, saying it was for Shelley's own protection. What did they think she needed protection from?

Dad didn't say much. He was watchful but silent. He seemed to be there more for moral support, but didn't pressure her like the others.

She'd managed to fend them all off. Trying to convince them everything was alright, she promised to keep in touch daily to let them know how she was coping. When they finally left, exhaustion set in.

So this morning, when the doorbell shrilled, she thought of hiding. Instead, she managed to pry herself from beneath the covers. There followed a deafening knock, and then someone glued their finger to the button for the bell. The noise nearly knocked her back onto the mattress.

She grabbed her dirty clothes from the floor, right where she'd dropped them the night before. "Hold your horses," she muttered, stumbling down the hall as the bell went again followed by heavy thumping on the door panel. She yanked it open.

Molly marched through looking like an angry bulldog, a frown on her face and a sheaf of papers in her hand. "'Bout time," she said, taking a seat at the kitchen counter. She adjusted her plaid skirt about her legs and propped her sandals on the foot rest. "I've been knocking for ten minutes."

Shelley rolled her eyes and closed the door. "I was sleeping. You didn't have to wake me."

Her friend gave her a hard look. "Yes, I did. I needed to get your attention. There are decisions to be made."

"There are?" Confused, she took a seat beside her. "What's going on? Is it something to do with the newspaper?"

"Yeah, kind of." Molly got a sly look in her eyes.

"Well, tell me."

"Better make some coffee first. I want you wide awake for this."

Shelley shuffled to the sink and pour water into the carafe, flicking on the machine. As she measured the coffee grounds into the filter, she glanced back at Molly. She had a determined look on her face which told her something serious was going on.

With coffee finally poured, Shelley slid back onto the stool and leaned tiredly on her elbows. "Okay, fire away."

"I've been talking with Mr. Martell," Molly began.

"Mr. Martell?"

"Yeah, he teaches your Web Design class."

Shelley frowned. "I know that," she said irritably. "Why were you talking to him? I thought this was about the newspaper."

Molly gave her a sympathetic look. "Because he's one of the few nice professors we have, and he's interested in helping you."

Shelley stiffened and buried her nose in the coffee mug. Eventually the silence became too much, and she had to look up.

Molly was waiting to pounce. "He's talked to your other professors. One wouldn't cooperate. But the rest will work with you."

"Work with me how?" she muttered, starting to feel cornered.

"Work with you to save your term. If you get on board, you can probably pass four of your courses and the time won't be totally lost. I told him your boyfriend had disappeared and nobody knows where he's gone. Martell was sympathetic. He knows you have a history of good student work and says he can wait. You concentrate on the other three courses, and get them out of the way. He's willing to give you a chance to get your feet under you again before you have to take his exam. He said he'd come up with something."

Shelley flailed around for an answer. She didn't care any more about her classes. But even if she did, why would she work on this plan? It just seemed so pointless. Hadn't she always done the reading, finished the labs, handed in the assignments, studied for exams? So what? She was in this Neverland of nothingness. It didn't matter any more.

"Thanks, Molly. That's good of you and Mr Martell to put together this..." She gestured vaguely at the papers lying on the counter. "But really... I don't think it's going to make a difference one way or the other."

Molly gave her a disbelieving look. "Of course, it'll make a difference. Why wouldn't it? You're almost at the end of your term, you can take an extra course or something to make up the lost credits..."

"It doesn't matter, Molly. I'm quitting." She took another sip of coffee. She'd finally said it out loud and it felt right. Just quit. Why fight it any longer? It was a relief to give up.

Molly turned slowly on the stool until she was facing her, eyes blazing. "No way are you going to quit. No way. That

123

asshole Billy Zach doesn't have that much power. Don't give him that power," she pleaded.

Molly's brow furrowed as she paused to catch her breath. "Now, have a look at what we've done." She grabbed the sheaf of papers and determinedly dragged them across the counter. "Here are the four courses you can rescue. This is what has to be done." Her finger jabbed at spots on the page as she talked.

Molly had always been one to set a goal and go after it and she didn't seem ready to back down now. She pointed to the notes from each professor. "Here's a list of the number of classes left in the term." The list was short, classes were almost over. There followed details of assignments, and dates for completion. Mr. Martell had shuffled all the Web Design handouts to the back, placing them at the end of the line.

"I'll be with you all the way, Shelley. I won't let you give up like this. Everyone has tough times, you know that. Mr. Martell says…"

Shelley couldn't take any more. She began to cry and as the tears ran down her cheeks, Molly wrapped an arm around her shoulders and kept talking. "Martell insists you come and see him today so he can iron out any problems in the plan. He's going to make it work."

Shelley hurt as if she'd taken a blow to the heart. First her family, now her friend. Maybe she wasn't such a freak after all.

Chapter Twenty-Six

Now...

Chris arrived at Shelley's place a little early. He was eager to get inside. Max met him at the fence and *woofed* softly, then galloped around to sniff his loafers as he came through the gate into the yard. He shuffled his bags into one hand and reached down to give the beast a rub.

His gaze travelled toward the light pouring through the glass doors in her suite. He heard an object hit the floor with a thud, and some low words that followed. He grinned. Probably a good thing he couldn't hear that. Didn't want to embarrass her.

He moved forward and spotted Shelley standing at the stove stirring something in a pot, the lid lying on the floor at her feet. She reached to adjust the temperature knob as he tapped on the glass. She startled and whirled around, panic on her face and a wooden spoon in her hand dripping some kind of sauce onto the floor.

She wore a low-cut wine-coloured blouse of a gauzy fabric that tied at the waist, and a pair of tight jeans. It made a very enticing package. His mouth watered.

As she opened the door, sliding it back gently on the new tracks, he stepped into the room. A wonderful aroma of tomato sauce and garlic rose from the stove. The table was set for two with paper napkins and glass goblets.

He handed her a bunch of flowers and watched her cheeks flush. "Oh, they're lovely," she said, her dark eyes shining. She reached for a glass vase in the cupboard above her head and he grabbed it down for her. His chest grew tight.

He laid his other package on the counter. "Something smells awfully good," he said, peering into the pot and giving it a stir. A second large pot of water boiled gently at the back.

"Spaghetti?" he asked. "I'm starved." It wasn't just dinner he was starved for, but he was willing to be patient.

"Yes. Won't be too long." She smiled. Snipping a bit off the bottom of the flower stems, she placed the lilies in the vase, adding greenery around them. She glanced at the parcel on the counter. "What did you bring?" she asked.

"Dessert," he said.

"Really?" Her face lit up. "I didn't have time to worry about dessert."

"It's just some brownies from the bakery."

"Ohhh, I love brownies."

He grinned and opened the paper bag, pulling out a couple of preserving jars. "Here's some jam Mum sent over. Raspberry and blackberry."

She stared at the jars in wonder, then picked one up to examine it. "Your mother made these? They look fabulous."

He took it from her hand and set it down on the counter. "You look fabulous," he said and lowered his mouth over hers. She stilled for a moment, then her lips parted and let him in. Right from the start he was on fire. He wrapped his arm around her, placing the other hand on her cheek as he deepened the kiss. She tasted sweet, she tasted like more. A lot more.

Something hissed on the burner and Shelley pulled out of his grasp.

"Uh..." She reached to grab the handle of the pot, then dropped it back on the stove, gasping as she shook her hand.

Chris turned the knob off and wrapped his fingers in the bottom of his shirt, nudging the pot off the burner.

"How's your hand?" He anxiously examined the red mark. It didn't look too bad, but was obviously hurting her. "Let's put some ice on it to cool it down."

"Yes, good idea." Her voice sounded weak.

He examined her pale cheeks. She'd better not faint on him. He had bigger plans for the evening. "Maybe sit here." He pulled a chair out and helped her to it, then found ice in the freezer to wrap in a tea towel. "There, hold it on your hand for a bit. Come here," he said, urging her off the chair again. He sat down and pulled her onto his knee, putting his arms around her. She leaned against his shoulder.

That was better. In fact, it felt fantastic. He rocked her against his chest, feeling the fragile bones under the tender skin. She wasn't very big, never had been. Her skin was like silk and her curves were pressed against him in an enticing fashion. The blouse had pulled open and the sight of the tops of her breasts made him go weak in the knees, but rigid in other parts of his body.

Pressing her head against his shoulder, he kissed her cheek and the corner of her mouth. "Oh, baby, you just light me up."

When next he lifted his head, she sagged against him, panting softly. He kissed her again, because he could. He was losing focus and had to shift her off his knee before he went too far. He was pretty sure she wasn't ready for that.

"Should we have dinner?" he asked. "I'm getting side-tracked here."

She laughed softly. "My hand is feeling better."

"Good. That's good. I think it was the kisses."

She giggled.

"I'll put the spaghetti on to boil," he said.

"Thank you." Shelley unwrapped the sodden towel and examined her palm. The red mark had faded to a rosy tone, exactly matching the colour of her mouth from all his attentions.

"That looks better. Sit up to the table and I'll have dinner ready in a minute."

"I'm supposed to be doing that," she protested.

He laughed and gave her a gentle shove with his hip. "My turn."

By the time they'd eaten she was back to laughing and teasing him. The nervousness and panic that had been evident upon his arrival seemed to have vanished.

"I'll wash," he said, rising to his feet. "The men always wash."

"Are you grumbling?" She stacked the plates. "Your mum explained to me that the men have to do the clean-up. It's some kind of Wright tradition."

"Right or Wright?" he asked with a laugh. "A tradition anyway." He filled the sink with soapy water. "This'll be easy. You put the food away."

As she slid the last pot into the sink, he turned and placed wet hands on her waist. The gauze of her blouse became translucent from the water.

"Kiss me, Shelley," he said. "I'm going to be away for a long time." She turned her sweet mouth up to his and grabbed hold of his shoulders. Lord, it felt like he'd been waiting for her his whole life. Maybe he had.

He placed one hand on her breast, that firm round mound that had been enticing him all evening. She gasped into his mouth and he massaged her, rubbing the turgid nipple under his thumb. His other hand slid down her waist and over her hip to haul her up against him. He was heavy and hard with need.

"Shelley, come play with me," he said.

She kissed his neck and he went up in flames.

Chapter Twenty-Seven

When Shelley pulled away from his caress and sat up, Chris shifted on the cushions of her couch. He watched with regret as she tugged her blouse closed and those delectable mounds disappeared from sight. He wasn't near ready to end this encounter.

"I'm not in a position to get involved with you," she said, glancing away.

He groaned and sat up. "I thought you were just in the perfect position to get involved." He ran a finger down the silky skin of her chest, pushing the fabric open again. "I can't get enough of you."

Her hands tightened, tying the blouse closed. "I'm serious, Chris. I remember you from grade six."

He sat up straighter and looked her in the eye. "I thought you did."

"I just didn't want to admit it, because…" Her fingers played with the tie belt.

"You were hoping I'd go away."

Her gaze darted up to meet his as she shook her head.

"Or you were *afraid* I'd go away." He raised her face to his with the pad of his thumb beneath her chin. "I'm not going anywhere, Shelley. Yes, I go off to work, but then I come home. Every time." He thought about the stretch he'd spent touring Europe. If he did that again, it would be because Shelley came with him.

"I know you lost Billy. It was sudden, and although it was a long time ago, there haven't been any answers for you." His heart hurt at the lost look on her face. Was she still mourning the bastard? "Doesn't mean you can't ever take another chance."

"I'm not waiting for him to return," she said, glancing sideways at him. "I was almost ready to walk away myself by the time he left. But with the police coming around now, and this new witness they claim to have found... It's all so frightening."

He pulled her against his chest, where she fit perfectly. "All the more reason to let me in," he said. "Then you're not facing this alone. I know you have your dad and sister, but maybe I can help, too. For one thing, I don't think you should talk to the police by yourself. You need protection. Get a lawyer and let him talk to them for you."

She stared at him as a tear slid down her cheek. "But I haven't done anything wrong! He left me, dumped me like I was worthless, and walked away!"

"Ah." He kissed her again, on her mouth until she stopped trembling, then along her jaw. "But you're not worthless. You're valuable, priceless. And he was a bastard. Who knows why he did what he did? But he can't hurt you any more, not if you don't let him."

He lowered his voice and ran a hand up her spine. "Don't let him hurt you, baby. Let me in. Give us a chance."

She relaxed against him and he gave an internal sigh. He was still fighting Billy, after all this time.

* * *

"A movie?"

Chris nodded and pushed Max out of the way to get closer to her. "Yeah. There's a new Superman movie out. Well, not that new, but I don't get to see most of these in Saudi Arabia. They're usually banned."

She laughed up at him, her eyes shining. "Seriously?"

"Have you seen it?" he teased. "I'll bet you haven't."

He was right. She didn't often go to the movies, but if she did it wasn't to see films like *Superman*. "Well…"

He was reading her expression. "See? I knew you'd like the idea." He took her hand and pulled her against him. As he laid his lips over hers, she sank into the kiss. She'd been busy all day, hadn't had time to exchange more than a few text messages with him. She missed him, missed this. Oh, she was in such deep trouble. But it was surprising how comfortable she was with this trouble. It had been a long time, and she was falling in love.

"Okay," she murmured against his mouth. "I could watch Superman."

She felt his smile, but got distracted by his big hands as they travelled over her body. He was breathing heavily and his erection pressed against her hip. He was as excited as she was.

She pulled back as he ran his palm across her cheek. "We need to get going or we'll miss the beginning of the movie, won't we?" she said. "And next time I get to choose which show we see. It's called sharing."

He laughed and held her jacket for her. It had been a mild day, but looked like it was about to turn colder. Typical March weather on the west coast.

Halfway through the show, with Superman doing super things on the huge screen, her cell phone buzzed. Shelley quickly grabbed it and shut off the sound as others glared toward them in the dark. "Sorry," she whispered and tucked it back in her purse. It vibrated, then again. She waited, having trouble focussing on the movie now. Another vibration, then two more in a row. Something was going on.

Surreptitiously, she pulled it out of the pocket of her handbag, pressing the button to turn it on. Chris immediately leaned over and cupped it with his hands to keep the screen light from annoying the people around them. "What is it?" he whispered. "An emergency?"

She nodded and peeked at the screen. A text from Lily, six texts from Lily. She clicked on the first one.

Talked to my PI, it said. *They've found a body.*

Chapter Twenty-Eight

"A body? Where?" Shelley stood in the lobby of the movie theatre, physically vibrating as she waited for her sister to answer. "How would it be linked to Billy after all this time?"

There was silence for a moment. "I'm just asking, hold on," Lily said. Then, "They found his ID, a driver's licence or something."

"My God." Shelley covered her mouth with her fingers and glanced up at Chris, hovering in front of her. "Where was it?" Her voice shook.

"Come home," Lily said. "I'll tell you what I know."

"Okay." She clicked the phone off and stared at Chris. "Can we go to Dad's house? I need to hear what's happened and where the police are going with this."

"Of course," he said. "Let's go. So where was the body?" He took her hand and walked out the exit doors of the movie theatre.

"I don't know." She rushed, trying to keep up with his long-legged stride.

"Odd that it would be found now, just when the police have a new witness," he remarked. "Seems kind of unreal."

* * *

A well-dressed stranger was sitting in the living room with Dad. He turned guardedly as Shelley entered, and she recognized him. Detective Helms, back with more questions no doubt. And where was Lily?

"Dad?" She walked over to his chair. "What's going on? Why did you let him in?"

Her father was pale and breathing heavily into his oxygen mask. "I didn't let him in," he wheezed. "He just knocked, and then came in. I thought it was you. Lily called and said she'd be a few minutes."

Shelley turned to the cop. "You can't do that. You can't just barge into our house and keep pestering us."

Hems stood, looming over her. "I have a few more questions, Ms. Blake. Do you think you and your father can answer them here or should we take you down to the station to be questioned? We've had another development in the case."

She blinked. "The case? How is this a case? Billy Zach walked away. He left."

Helms shook his head. "We have a body now. And Zach's ID was at the scene. We definitely have a case."

Shoulders shaking, she glanced toward the door. Chris had parked his truck and was coming up the steps. "Where was it?" Her voice was little more than a whisper.

"I can't tell you that at present." The cop glanced at Chris as he came through the door and turned to Dad. "Mr. Blake, would you mind answering some questions for me?"

Chris stepped through the entrance, shot a look at her father, then focussed on Helms. "I think everyone here has decided they're not going to answer any more questions without a lawyer present. So, when they have someone lined up, they'll let you know," he said.

Shelley took a deep breath as relief flowed through her. "Yes," she said. "That's right. Isn't it, Dad? We'll get a lawyer."

Helms shrugged. "You'll still have to answer the questions."

"I don't see why," Shelley shot back. "We don't know anything, we haven't done anything. Just because we knew Billy, doesn't mean we have evidence to add to your case."

Dad gave her a weak grin, and her heart gave a frightened thump. He looked different, worse than before. Instead of flushed, he looked washed out, his face pale as paper. His breathing sounded painful and laboured.

"I'm asking you to leave now, Detective Helms." Shelley moved to stand by the front door. "Please phone ahead next time. I think we've been more than patient."

Jaw tight, Helms walked out and down the steps.

Shelley closed the door with a sharp click and turned the lock. "Dad." She crossed the room and knelt in front of his chair. "I think we should go to the hospital. You don't look well, and I don't know how to adjust your oxygen. You need medical attention."

He shook his head, glancing down to fiddle with the tank feed attached to his chair. "I'm fine," he panted. "I just need to get this thing working properly." He flailed at the knobs, a rattle starting in his chest.

"Mr. Blake." Chris squatted in front of his chair to speak to him. "You should go to the hospital. If you pass out, you can't tell them what care you need, or what your symptoms are. I'm going to call an ambulance." He reached for his cell phone as Dad gazed at him with a startled expression on his face.

Then he nodded, and took Shelley's hand. "Okay," he gasped. "I guess that makes sense.

"Thanks, Dad." She held his hand until they heard the siren in the distance, then went to get his wallet and ID from the bedside table.

As the attendants strapped her father on the stretcher and carried him out to the ambulance, Shelley went around the house, locking the rest of the doors.

Where was Lily? She was the one who'd asked Shelley to come home in the first place. She was supposed to be here.

Chapter Twenty-Nine

Lily met them at the hospital, arriving in the emergency room in a full-blown panic.

"It's okay." Shelley dragged her away from Dad's stretcher, positioned in the hallway as they waited for medical attention. He'd been outfitted with an oxygen mask and breathing tubes and was sleeping in the midst of the turmoil swirling around him.

"He's all right. They say it's a temporary attack and his breathing has normalized. They're going to keep him in for observation. There might be something else they can do to help him get his oxygen supply under control."

As Lily calmed, Shelley studied the tall lean man at her side. This must be the private investigator who was feeding them all the information. It would be interesting to hear if he had anything new to say. Helms had already confirmed Lily's facts from earlier in the evening about a body turning up.

Chris leaned on the wall nearby, patiently waiting, muscled arms folded across his chest. He'd been calm and steady through the whole rigmarole of getting Dad to the hospital and having him admitted, keeping her from losing control. He was a steady guy, applying common-sense and a practical approach to all the upheaval that seemed to churn around her right now.

When had her life veered so far out of control? It was starting to feel remarkably like the time after Billy disappeared. The thought frightened her out of her wits.

She turned back to her sister. "We went to the house to talk to you, Lily. You said you'd meet us there."

"Yeah," Lily shrugged. "You got there before we could. Then I got your message about taking Dad to the hospital. Sort of knocked me for a loop." She gave a sickly smile.

The fellow beside her put out his hand. "I'm James. I've been supplying a bit of information to Lily, but it's best if the police don't know where it comes from. Best for me and my future career." He grinned and shook her hand. "Can we sit down somewhere? I'd like to fill you in."

Chris stepped forward and pointed to a small alcove near the entry. "We could try there."

James settled into a chair only after seating Lily next to him. He seemed quite taken with her sister. Was this the reason they were getting so much inside information from him?

"They found a body," he began. "There was a leather jacket at the site, which was still in reasonable shape. Leather tends to age better than cloth or other types of fabric. The wallet in the pocket contained a number of items that were badly degraded, but the driver's licence is made of plastic and stood up well. It was identifiable as that of William Zach. They still have to do some more work to make sure the body matches the identification—dental records, DNA, stuff like that. They're trying to locate the parents to get the information they need."

Shelley took a shallow breath and felt a warm hand on her arm. Chris leaned into her side, and just the solid feel of him helped her calm down.

"Where did they find this body?" he asked.

James turned to him. "There's been some work done on the old road past Sooke Lake and behind the dam. It runs off Humpback Road through the closed gold mine to the back of Shawnigan Lake. They found the body in a shallow grave at the side of the road. No way to know how long it's been there or when it was placed there. There's never much traffic through that route, you have to have four-wheel drive and up till now the road has been almost impassable."

"Humpback Road?" Shelley darted a glance at her sister. "Didn't Dad…" She shut up as Lily gave a sharp shake of her head.

What was she thinking? She was starting to lose all common sense. Sometimes Dad drove that way as a short cut to his work camp. But she didn't need to broadcast that information, and his work camps had shifted to numerous locations over all the time he'd worked up-island. She hadn't a clue what years he drove the Malahat and what years he drove around the reservoir into the back of the Shawnigan district.

She closed her eyes and prayed for a clear head. Things were bad enough without her putting her foot in it.

She looked at James and caught his last comments about the forensic work still to be done to confirm the identity of the body. "The body's that of a male," he added, "fairly young, about five feet nine inches tall. That's all they know at the moment."

Shelley took a breath and held it. That was Billy's height. Was Dad involved in this after all? It was too frightening to contemplate.

She waited for the nausea to pass.

Then…

It had been a week since Molly knocked on her door. It wasn't getting any easier to climb out of bed after another sleepless night. But Shelley knew if she didn't leave the apartment, it was guaranteed nothing would get done. So she made the decision to attend the campus every day, whether she had classes or not. She'd work in the library or one of the cafeterias instead of staying home.

And if she didn't get up and out, she'd discovered it was also guaranteed someone would phone to check on her, knowing she still lay in bed. Today it was her sister Lily, calling before she headed off to school. She didn't talk long because she had a class starting soon, but she sounded so cheerful Shelley couldn't help feeling encouraged.

She gave herself ten minutes to shower and dress, ten minutes to have a bite of breakfast and five more minutes to find her pack and keys and escape out the door. She was sure she looked a mess, but at the moment that didn't seem very important.

This morning when she descended to the parking lot, a frowning Molly was leaning against the fender of her car. When she spotted Shelley, her eyes lit up. "Great guns," she exclaimed. Molly had always loved that expression. Lord knew where it came from.

She gave Shelley a hug, wished her a good day and headed toward her own car parked nearby. Shelley realized her friend had waited to see if she left in the morning. It made her cry to think about it. Molly was a good friend. At that moment, she loved and hated her in equal measure for being such a thorn in her side. But mostly she loved her.

As she walked away, Molly tossed a comment over her shoulder. "Come by the newspaper office today. We're going to run an article on the university president and his fake credentials."

With her mouth open, Shelley watched her friend leave. They were always digging up dirt on someone. Molly had guts, she was the one with enough nerve to do an exposé like that. It made Shelley laugh, the first time in weeks.

That day she spent three solid hours in the library without a break, then had a bite of lunch in the cafeteria and went back at it. She got a lot done—sorting and researching notes for the term paper on Overseas Marketing. She'd narrowed down her thesis and the conclusions she hoped to prove. Now she just had to get started on writing it, with the goal of being finished by the end of the week. Even so, she'd be barely within the deadlines of the plan that Martell had organized with the other professors.

Billy was so good at this kind of stuff. He used to help outline and establish her thoughts when she was writing her term papers. Suddenly tears ran down her cheeks and she had to hide out in the washroom until she recovered her equilibrium. The problem was, his parents had removed any illusions she might have had about their son.

His mother was alive and well. So, what was he crying about all that time? Were they fake tears, designed to manipulate her when he discovered her mother died while she was in high school?

Everything she believed about him had turned out to be false. His father laughed when she mentioned the second-year university courses Billy had taken. He sneered that she knew nothing about his son.

Billy had played her for a fool and she'd fallen for every lie, every fabrication. What did that make her?

Her chest hurt all the time now, just like that night Billy hit her with his fist.

Chapter Thirty

Now...

Chris felt panic set in. "I'll email," he said. "I'll text you if the texts will go through. Sometimes there are problems. The phone companies have had ongoing trouble with service in Arab countries. But email has worked fine the whole time I've been there." Seated on Shelley's couch, he knew time was running out. It was tearing at his nerves.

Shelley shivered as he gathered her close against his chest. "I can't believe you're leaving already," she said.

He cupped her head with his hand, cradling her against him. "I know. It always goes much faster than I think it will. Don't know why that is—some kind of time-space continuum process, perhaps." He grinned at her confused expression. "I read too many science fiction novels."

He rubbed the loose strands of her hair between his fingers. "I've always loved your hair."

She stilled for a moment. "You used to play with my braids."

"I know." He gave faint smile. "The colour fascinated me, almost black but not quite, and it was so soft. It got my little heart all excited to play with those braids."

"I used to wonder if you were putting glue on them."

He leaned down to peer into her face. "Really? I wouldn't."

"I know that now." She gave him a smirk.

"Well, tell me this," he said. "Why were your braids military straight one day and all over the place the next?"

"Oh," she tipped her face up to his. "When Mum did them, they were straight. But if she was too sick, Grams did it and she wasn't very good at it. Her kids were all boys."

He ran a finger across her soft mouth. "I'm sorry about your mum. That's so hard. I've been very lucky with my folks. How's your dad doing?"

Her mouth turned down. "This morning they said they're going to send him home soon. There'll be a community nurse checking on him a couple of times a day. They said he won't get any better, but likely worse before too long."

"Huh." He leaned his temple against the side of her head and just held her for a moment. "Did you know the police forensics did an examination of my truck?"

She turned her head to gaze up at him wordlessly.

"I don't know what they thought they'd find, but I got a call yesterday to say I was free and clear. They didn't find any evidence."

She glanced down. "It's embarrassing. Because you know me, you've been dragged into this whole scenario as some kind of a suspect."

He shrugged. "It doesn't matter. Shelley, I wish I didn't have to go. I hate leaving you. Did you call that lawyer I found for you?"

"Not yet, but I will," she promised.

He huffed out a breath. "If the police come back, don't talk to them. Make sure Lily knows, too. Hopefully they won't bother your father while he's in the hospital."

She sighed and kissed the side of his throat. The V neck of her blouse sagged open to reveal the smooth skin at the tops of her breasts.

He froze for a second, then shifted to lay his mouth over hers. Her lips were so tender and warm, she just pulled him

142

in. He was falling fast. His chest became tight and his breathing laboured. He kissed her again, thrusting his tongue into her mouth, exploring those hidden depths.

"Shelley," he groaned, running his tongue along her throat, heading for the sight he'd just captured as her blouse sagged further. "I want you. I don't want to scare you, but…."

"I know," she murmured.

He glanced at her face. "Yeah, I guess you do." He gave a self-deprecating grin. "Pretty obvious, huh?"

"I want you too." When she looked into his eyes, with that sweet smile on her lovely mouth, his heart thumped unevenly in his chest.

She rose and took his hand. "Come with me."

Anticipation rising in his belly, he quickly heaved himself off the couch. Oh, he'd come all right. If he could make that happen, he'd be a happy man. Was he finally getting somewhere with her? He'd know soon enough, but her invitation left him short of breath.

* * *

Standing in the doorway to her room, nerves suddenly took root in her stomach. Her hands were cold and she began to shake. What had she started? He was leaving tomorrow and she'd be alone again.

Chris's warm hand closed around her shoulder and he drew her against him. "It's okay, Shelley. We don't have to make love if you're not ready." There were brackets of tension around his wide expressive mouth.

She looked up into his bright blue eyes. Was she ready? It had been so long, she didn't even know any more what ready might feel like. She'd never know if she didn't take this step. And he was the only man she trusted.

She pressed against his body, burying her nose in the soft cotton shirt covering that hard chest and took a deep breath, savouring his scent. She trusted everything about him. Why was she hesitating now? She'd already wrestled this decision to the ground, and here it was again, rearing a whole slew of ugly fears that she thought she'd defeated earlier.

Chris wasn't Billy, he wouldn't sleep with her then leave. Although that's what he'd already explained he was going to do—leave tomorrow morning. But that was different, a job she'd known about since she met him again in the Ministry office that fateful day.

He tilted her face to meet his. "It's alright," he said. "I just need a kiss." His warm mouth descended over hers and she stood on tiptoe to receive him. Longing bloomed in her breast. This was what she yearned for, why hesitate? Time was running out.

She gasped into his mouth as his big hand wrapped around her breast and carefully squeezed. A fire lit in her belly. His erection pressed against her hip and she rocked gently, feeling the size and hardness there. He froze for a second, holding his breath.

"Shelley, I'm pretty uncomfortable here. Maybe we should just go back to the couch." He tried to grin but it looked like more of a grimace.

"I don't think so," she said. This time there was no hesitation. She pulled him all the way into her room and backed him up against the side of the mattress. Then she began undoing the buttons on his shirt. He started to laugh as his hands got in her way, roaming over her body. Finally, he hauled her against him and fell backward onto the bed. The mattress squeaked.

A hiccup started in her throat, small breathless laughter that grew until she lay on the long length of him, helplessly giggling into his half-buttoned shirt. Chris's chest heaved beneath her and he ran his hands down her back, pausing when he gripped her bottom and pressed himself against her.

Her laughter died as suddenly as it had begun.

"Chris?"

"Yes, baby. I'm right here and I'm not going anywhere."

"I know," she said. "I'm sure."

He made a choking sound and dumped her on her back, wrestling with the closure on her slacks. "I just need to get you out of these clothes and we can take it slow from there."

"Oh, of course." She fumbled to find the tab of the zipper.

"Never mind." He brushed her hands away. "I want to do it. It's my job."

She paused, remembering he'd said the same thing when he'd held the door to the coffee shop for her. It was his job. He'd do it and she didn't have to.

A sob burst from her throat and she wrapped her arms around his head. He leaned in to press a tender kiss to her breast through the blouse. It eased a hard knot that lingered there, soothed something in her soul.

"Chris?" she asked.

"Hmm." She felt the button give as her zipper slid down. Then he was tugging her slacks off her legs and there was no need for more words. Her blouse had disappeared, her bra sagged as he unsnapped it. His own clothes disappeared in a rush and he was back on the bed, hands everywhere, smoothing her skin and reshaping it for the attention of his mouth and tongue. A hum started in her throat, a song of pleasure and joy. No tears now, just a wild eagerness as he carefully made a place for himself between her legs.

When he entered her, there was a jolt of something almost otherworldly, something hot and jubilant, overwhelming. The hair on his broad chest abraded her skin, making her nipples even harder as they rubbed against him. He groaned, moving slowly against her, inside her, as the pleasure gathered and mounted.

Why had she waited so long for this? She tried to breathe but then forgot as he pressed further inward, his lips roaming her cheek, then back to her mouth. His kisses were soothing and demanding, hungry and fulfilling.

Her climax caught her unawares, hurling her over some barrier that she'd hidden behind for too long, propelling her far out above the land. She floated effortlessly, dimly aware of a heavy grunt and long groan as Chris slowly collapsed on top of her. He slid to the side, dragging her with him until she landed gently on his chest.

Now she knew why she'd waited. It wasn't why but who she'd waited for. She'd been asking the wrong question.

Chapter Thirty-One

Chris left Shelley's place at five in the morning. He had to pack his gear at his parent's home and tidy up some loose ends before heading to the airport. He glanced at the clock on the dashboard. Should be okay for time.

His first flight from Victoria to Vancouver was a short twenty-minute hop across the Strait of Georgia. The second, from Vancouver to Montreal, was almost five hours with a two-hour stopover before his next flight. It was the third leg of the journey that was long—seven hours to Frankfurt, Germany. After that, another five and a half hours to Jeddah.

He knew he'd sleep. Travelling first class made it easy anyway, but he was worn out, in the best possible way. His legs felt weak.

The look of satisfaction on his face would probably give him away. Better not let Mum see that. He knew his parents would be there to send him off and Dad would insist on driving him to the terminal. That's just who they were.

Then there was Shelley, of the great dark eyes and loose soft hair. He'd had the best night of his life. When she took his hand and led him into her soft-smelling room, he thought his heart would stop. The whole experience was magical—dim movement and small sounds. The moment he entered her, feeling her wet and ready, the slip and slide, had been totally overwhelming. He'd been in some kind of altered state—watching her sweet face, those beautiful eyes half closed, feeling her nails digging into his back…

Abruptly he pulled over to the side of the road and jammed his foot on the brake, coming to a quick stop. He needed to get himself under control, pay attention to what he was doing. He had to take care of a few things and get ready for his job before he left.

Easing his tires back onto the road, he watched the night sky fade from black to steel grey. His thoughts drifted back to leaving Shelley's place. She'd walked him to the door in her thin nightie, her dark hair flowing down her back. He'd leaned into her kiss, totally replete for once in his life. He might never need sex again.

He laughed softly as he braked to turn into his parent's driveway. Who was he kidding? He'd need her again as soon as he caught his breath. By then he'd be halfway between here and Jeddah, travelling in the wrong direction. Was it time to have another look at his lifestyle? Because three months without her was going to be hell on wheels.

Shelley was in a tough spot, her mother gone early and her father ill. It was a much different life for her than the one he'd led. This situation of Billy Zach, and a body turning up now was just another difficult dimension added to the mix. He hated to leave—it was the worst possible time to go.

He didn't know what information the police had about Billy's death. When the guy had first disappeared, everyone assumed he'd just taken off. Wouldn't be the first time a man ran when he was getting in too deep with a woman, or looking criminal charges in the face.

Chris had tried to keep a close eye on things since then. Occasionally there'd been something in the paper, and to his vast relief, Rob always saved it to pass on to him. He'd known of Chris's early and continuing interest in Shelley Blake.

The thing was, there'd been no information. Nothing to go on. The parents hadn't seemed too upset, weren't demanding action from the police. He'd wondered if perhaps the police figured Billy was in touch with Mr. and Mrs. Zach, given they weren't all over them about the case, didn't seem anxious to find their son.

This new information changed all that. The police were obviously thinking more and more that this was a case of murder. Billy never showed up again because he couldn't.

Chris knew neither Shelley nor her sister had been involved in his disappearance. Were the police looking at their father?

He remembered how he'd felt about Billy at university. He'd had a strong urge to make Billy disappear when he saw what the relationship had been like between him and Shelley, and Chris wasn't her dad. A father would have some pretty strong urges, too.

He didn't know how this would pan out, or who the police might target as a suspect. Mr Blake looked pretty weak today but had still been working in the bush four years ago. Anyone doing that kind of work had to be physically strong.

On the other hand, there must have been a whole line-up of guys who had wanted to settle a score with Billy Zach.

* * *

Shelley came awake slowly and lay luxuriating in the tangled sheets. The bedding smelled of Chris and sex. Her heart gave a jump and settled into an irregular beat. She'd done it. She'd gotten involved.

Giggling, she rolled to her back, sliding the pillow under her head. She felt like a different woman. Was this a new life? It would take a while to discover that. She placed her palms on her breasts. They were a little tender this morning, as were some other parts of her body. Tender but not sore, just had received a lot of very loving attention. She hummed to herself.

Chris was leaving this morning, and wouldn't be back for three months. She stilled, absorbing the ramifications of that. He'd taken care of everything he could while he was still here.

The gate in her fence worked now, her entry door slid open with the push of a hand. He'd changed the oil in her car, not that she knew it was needed. He'd helped her buy a new laptop and installed all the software she used for her business and newsletters.

More importantly, he'd taken charge and called an ambulance when Dad had his attack. And he'd informed the police the family would only speak to them with a lawyer present.

She glanced at the night table where a piece of paper was pinned under the water glass. It contained information on the lawyer he'd recruited for her. All she had to do was call him.

Why was she putting it off? Because once she called a lawyer, she was acknowledging, even if only to herself, that someone in the family might be involved in the death of Billy Zach and needed the legal services on offer.

She sighed and sat up. Dad was coming home today from the hospital and she had to go over there and spend some time getting ready for his return. She'd call the lawyer first.

Russell Brewster was in court but she left a message and he phoned her back before she left the house.

"Just call me Russ," he said. "Everyone does. Chris is a long-time friend of mine and he told me you might call. How do you know him?"

Shelley laughed lightly. "I've known him since grade six." Her face was suddenly hot, but she hoped her embarrassment didn't come through in her voice.

Russ chuckled. "Well, you've got me beat there. What can I help you with? I don't do solicitor's work—wills and estates, property transfers, stuff like that, if that's what you're looking for."

"No, this is something different," she said. "I had a boyfriend at university who disappeared without leaving any information behind. He was never seen again. We all assumed he'd run off." She choked for a moment. It was harder to talk about this than she'd imagined it would be. It was still a very emotional issue.

"Anyway, that was four years ago. The police have reopened the file, because they say they have a new witness, and now a body has been found with indications it might be him."

"Huh. Just a minute." There was a click and muffled voices. Then he came back on the phone. "Sorry, just checking something. So, do the police want to talk to you?"

"They've talked to me a couple of times recently. They've also talked to my father. We need your help."

"Sounds good. Why don't you come into the office, say tomorrow afternoon? Bring your father. I'll see you then and we can sort something out."

"Thank you." She thought she might collapse with relief. "Thank you so much."

"You're welcome." She heard a smile in his voice. "I can't promise anything, but we'll do our best."

"Yes. That's exactly what we need, your best."

Chapter Thirty-Two

Then...

Shelley was excited. Finally, finally, she was graduating! It was overwhelming, yet almost a let-down after everything that had happened leading up to this day.

She'd taken an extra course last term and now would finish with the rest of her class. It wasn't even that much of a stretch. She was used to the heavy work load. Her employers at the pharmacy were excited for her and she'd had no trouble cutting back her hours of work when needed to attend to other matters.

Everyone was coming to the grad ceremony. Dad arrived home early from camp and bought himself a new jacket to wear, an unheard of event. He was so proud of her. He'd rented a van with a handicap ramp so Grams could come. Grams was in the care home but delighted to attend.

Shelley stopped by the house that morning to find Lily jumping up and down with excitement. She answered the door wearing her housecoat, hair wrapped in a towel. "I've been bragging to all my friends," she said. "You're graduating! This is so exciting."

Shelley laughed and gave her a hug, noticing anew that her younger sister was now taller than she was. When did that happen?

"Come and see my outfit," Lily declared. "I'm just not sure what to think. Is it too mature for me?" Her face wore a puzzled frown. She pointed to a hanger holding a dress and bolero in dark purple, the sleeves narrow and beaded.

"It's beautiful, Lily." Shelley looked into her worried eyes. "It's a perfect colour for you. You'll look gorgeous." Then she giggled. "Don't forget. I'll be up there sweating under the black gown and I'll have a permanent dent in my forehead from the cap."

Lilly smiled and hugged her again. There were tears in her eyes. "Even with a dent in your forehead, you're still the best sister a girl could have. Dad made reservations for us at the Chinese restaurant for tonight."

Later, at the ceremony, Shelley stood with the graduating crowd as the students walked across the stage one at a time to receive their degrees. The lights were too bright so she couldn't see into the audience, but when her name was called, she definitely heard Dad's deep voice and Lily's shrill one as they called her name.

She didn't cry. She'd finished with crying, but it was difficult to hold the tears back. Grams hugged her afterward. "Congratulations, sweetheart. You're the first one in the family with a university degree," she said. "But not the last." They both turned to smile at Lily.

Now...

Chris got off the plane in Jeddah in the shimmery heat and pulled out a pair of dark sunglasses. Everyone here wore them, summer and winter. It was too bright to avoid it. He grabbed his pack and walked out of the building to stand in the shade of the entrance.

He recognized the Asmira company bus, waiting in a long line of buses for the foreign workers arriving back after their scheduled breaks. He saw a few of the men from his crew already climbing on board. There were a lot of Indian and Philippino workers here, a few of them employed on his project, and a slew of engineers from Canada and the US. At four years employment, Chris was in the middle of the pack in terms of longevity. Some were just starting with Asmira Engineering, others had been here for a long time, finding the lifestyle suited them. Harvey, whose mother always talked to Mum about this place, was one of those. Apparently, he was going on eleven years and still loving it.

Chris stepped away from the door and into the sunlight. Immediately, he started to sweat. He'd grown to appreciate why the Arabs wore the robes and head covers that they did. It was like a system of insulation from the rays of the sun in an effort to keep cool.

He climbed on board the bus, took a rear seat and turned up the AC in the rack above his head. Best to take it slow. When he was at home, he settled quickly into the rhythm of life there. It was more energetic, focussed, and competitive. Stepping back into the traces here was sometimes a real stretch.

He worked out of the city of Riyadh on several projects. Right now, the focus was on completing the construction of an oil processing plant. The Arab work day was the normal eight hours, except during Ramadan when it changed to six. The usual weekend was Friday and Saturday, although the foreigners only got one day off.

Projects proceeded differently in Saudi than they did back home, with the chain of command often being interrupted here by what he saw as politics. And wasn't that why people travelled in the first place, to experience something different?

But living and working here took its own toll and Chris felt that with a vengeance on this return trip. He wanted to be back home. He was just getting started on a relationship with Shelley. How could he keep her happy from this distance? How to keep himself satisfied?

He gritted his teeth and glared out the window.

The bus lurched as another couple of guys climbed aboard. One of the men walked toward him down the aisle.

"Chris, how are you? You've been doing some travelling, right?"

He turned to find Harvey settling into the seat beside him as the bus driver started the engine and eased into traffic.

"Harvey. Were you just in Victoria?" He moved over, shifting his pack to the floor between his feet.

"No. Well, yes, but only for the first couple of weeks. I returned to Europe early. I've been in Italy the last few. Great place. Food's good. All the pasta made with Canadian wheat, eh?"

They grinned at the old story of how the famous Italian pasta was made with durum wheat grown on the plains of western Canada.

Harvey sighed and patted his chest, reaching for a cigarette package in his breast pocket that wasn't there. "Just quit smoking. Still trying to get used to it."

Chris glanced at him. "I can imagine. I'm glad I never started. Hard to give it up, eh?"

"Yeah. It's been a struggle, especially in Italy where there was someone with a cigarette in his mouth on every other street corner."

They bumped onto a side road that skirted the downtown of Jeddah. Harvey leaned closer. "How long do you think you'll work in this place?" he asked.

Chris looked at him. He couldn't decide if he was too frustrated to answer the question or not. "Don't know," he said noncommittally.

"I think I've had it." Harvey shifted and leaned his arm against the window.

Chris opened his mouth in surprise, then closed it. Harvey? The guy who promoted the heck out of what they did over here? "How so?" he asked. "This seems kinda sudden."

Harvey nodded. "Yeah. Maybe to you. But I've been thinking about quitting for a while now. Too much of a stretch to conform to the culture here every time I return. It's worn me out."

Chris nodded. He'd just been thinking the same thing. "I suppose," he said. "But then, where? Back to Canada? Most of those jobs are in the north, so totally different from this."

"Yeah, I had an interview while I was home this last time. A couple, actually. I've got a position waiting for me—northern Alberta and the North-West Territories. I only have one more three-month stint on my contract and then I'm a free man. And I don't have to sign a contract back in Canada. I'll do my job and if I don't like it, I'll find something else."

"I'm surprised," Chris said. "You've boasted for years that this is the best place to work." He glanced out the window, studying the sun as it lay low on the horizon. Once it went below that line it would be pitch black outside.

"I know," Harvey said. "Nothing like reinforcing your own decision."

"Yeah, that's true." He envied Harvey his freedom. Chris had more than three months left on his contract, and things were happening back home that he couldn't influence or control. It was damned irritating.

Chapter Thirty-Three

The handicap bus pulled up in front of the house and the back doors opened. Dad tried to wheel himself out onto the sidewalk but the driver moved to help as Shelley ran down the front steps.

She grabbed the handles of the wheelchair and waved her thanks to the driver. "Let's go this way," she said, manoeuvring Dad's chair up the walk to the side door where a ramp had been built last year. "Are you glad to be home?"

"You don't know the half of it," her father growled as he adjusted the knob on his oxygen feed. "Couldn't wait to get out of that place, with everyone rushing around and interfering, telling me what to do."

In the house, she wheeled him into the living room, taking a moment to get him situated and his gear put away in the bedroom. When she came back out, she gave him an uncertain look. "I've arranged some care for you, Dad. Lily can't handle everything herself and we shouldn't leave you without help. But you have to cooperate with me."

He eyed her guardedly. "You mean a nurse to come here and hold my hand?"

She bared her teeth at him. "Only if you want her to."

Dad laughed. "Okay. I'll cooperate. I know Lily's been overloaded, and you've got your business going there."

"Promise?"

At his nod, she gave a real smile. "Good. I've ordered some dinner to be delivered here tonight and Lily will be home with us. We can go from there."

"Yeah." He frowned and gave her a sideways glance. "You know I'm not going to get any better."

"Yes, Dad. The doctor already said." Tears popped into her eyes and she leaned against him, resting her arm on his heavy shoulder.

"Now, don't cry. We all have to go sometime," he said gruffly. "I need to take care of business, that's all. I've got a will, and there's the house…"

"I know," she sobbed. "But I don't want to see a will, or talk about who gets the house. I just want you here with us."

He wrapped an arm around her hip and rocked her against him. "All in good time," he said. "I've had a wonderful life with a beautiful wife and two lovely daughters. That's all there is to say. I'm proud of you girls." He pointed to the television. "Can you reach the remote for me?"

She picked it up from the end table and handed it to him. As he clicked the TV on, she said, "Just so you know, we have to go out tomorrow. We've got an appointment with a lawyer, someone Chris found for us. He's going to help with this issue of the police investigation."

Dad just nodded, his attention fixed on the screen.

* * *

The trip to the lawyer's office was all the more difficult because of Dad's condition. By the time the handicap bus service arrived at the house to pick them up, he was already short of breath, an attack that sounded like it might escalate into something much more serious.

"I'll go on my own, Dad," Shelley offered. "I'm going to call the nurse and get her over here. With Lily in the middle of an exam right now, we won't all be there anyway."

"No, I can manage," Dad gasped. "I need to talk to this pencil-pusher myself, make sure he knows what he's doing. I can't leave everything to you."

His breathing had calmed by the time they arrived at the old building downtown that housed the legal offices. A side entrance had a ramp leading into the main hall and around to the elevator doors.

Russell Brewster's office was on the third floor. His secretary greeted them, but a short stocky man soon appeared from a doorway behind her. "Shelley Blake," he said, shaking her hand. "Good to meet you. And this is your father. Just call me Russ."

Dad wheeled himself into the office and engaged the brake on his chair. "I'm Jerry Blake," he said. "We need to sort out this mess."

Russ nodded and pointed to a chair for Shelley, then seated himself behind his desk. "Tell me what's been going on," he said.

Shelley began the story, with Dad interrupting her every few minutes. His breathing sounded almost normal now, and she wondered why the symptoms seemed to come and go like that. At least it meant he got some relief from having to struggle for breath.

Russ made a few notes as they talked, then pulled up a screen on his laptop. "I've done a bit of research," he said. "Found old news reports, and such. Not too helpful. No one seemed to know anything about his disappearance at the time it happened."

Shelley nodded tightly. "Not even his parents. Once they'd emptied the apartment of his things, they took his Jeep and left. They didn't talk to me after that, not that I had anything of interest to tell them. Billy had left a note not to contact him, and I never heard from him again." She tried to keep her voice from shaking.

Russ gave her a long look. "You're aware Zach had quite a history with the police."

She glanced at Dad, then back at the lawyer. "I know that now. I didn't at the time."

Dad growled something under his breath.

She ignored him. "But what I need to find out is why the police keep coming back to talk to us. I'm afraid I might make a comment that will lead them in the wrong direction. I've made numerous statements, most of them right after Billy left. But they keep calling. They seem to think I had something to do with his disappearance."

Russ shrugged. "Stranger things have happened, I suppose. But assuming you didn't, there are others who might. Right, Jerry?"

Dad nodded and sat straighter in his chair. "That's for sure," he said.

Shelley glared at her father in astonishment. "Don't joke, Dad. This is serious."

He looked at the lawyer for a moment before he turned his head and said, "I know, sweetheart. Sorry."

Russ glanced down at his notes for a moment, tapping his pen on the desk. "There's been another development," he said at last. "I've been in contact with the police and asked them to channel any questions for you through my office."

He took a breath. "Some forensics has been returned and there were signs of paint on the leather jacket found with the body. Now, no one is saying how old those paint flecks are. Could have been there for a year before he disappeared. But the significant thing is this—it's paint from a black Ford pickup."

Chapter Thirty-Four

Shelley couldn't calm down. She had a newsletter due today, yet it was the last thing she wanted to attend to. She motored from stove to fridge to cupboard, wondering what to have for breakfast, then decided she didn't need any. It was too late, she'd slept in, and it would be lunch time soon so she'd eat then.

She let Max out into the yard, then checked her email. One from Chris. Eagerly she clicked on it. With the time difference, maybe all his messages would arrive in the morning.

What are you doing? I miss you.

She smiled as her chest grew tight. She missed him too, with an ache deep within. It had only been two days, or was it one? He'd left early in the morning, so should she count that day or...

I've just worked a ten-hour stint. Something went wrong with the structural beams and we had to re-do some of the specs.

The work he did overseas sounded so exciting. Would she ever get to see that, or visit him over there? It would be a stretch, her current workload was such that...

She whirled in frustration and plugged the kettle in. That newsletter wouldn't write itself, and if she got it in late she stood to lose the contract.

Opening her files to the document she'd started a few days ago, she began at the top, proofing what she'd already laid out. But her mind wouldn't stay on task.

What did Dad mean by his comments at the lawyer's office? He shouldn't play around with his words. It might lead people to think he'd had something to do with Billy's disappearance. Even though Russ was working for them, they couldn't mislead him. He needed to have all the facts to defend them, if it ever came to that.

Would it come to that? A flash of heat swamped her, and her ears rang. They were in so much trouble.

Lily, at least, had no part of this. She'd been fifteen and in grade ten at the time. No way could someone try to pin anything on her. That just left her and Dad.

Given she didn't do anything, did that mean Dad might have? He'd driven a black Ford truck. A shudder worked its way up her spine. It wasn't possible that he'd been involved. She was positive it had been a Sunday night, just after nine o'clock, when she'd arrived home to the empty apartment. Dad had already left for camp by that time, usually starting out around four or five in the afternoon. He wouldn't have been around to play a part in this whole debacle.

Pulling her attention back to work, she checked her file for the newsletter information she needed, and began outlining it on the page. There was a change in management at the Ministry that would go in the body of the document. There were a few minor policy reminders. Those could go in an itemized list down one side. She had done an interview of a department head, one of a half-dozen of interviews that she would be conducting over the next couple of months. She just needed the photo of the woman. Where was it?

As she clicked through a file of documents looking for the right picture, another thought entered her head that brought her up short.

It wasn't what time she'd gotten home to the apartment that night that was so important. It was what time she'd left. Because anything that happened had happened after she'd departed for work. She always left a half hour before her shift began. That day, her shift had started at five o'clock.

And there was paint from a black Ford pickup truck on Billy's jacket.

* * *

Shelley was breathing heavily by the time she returned from her run, Max trotting faithfully at her side. It had been dumping rain but she'd needed the exercise. With Chris gone, she felt very alone dealing with all the upheaval around her.

She had another AA meeting tonight, but the compulsion to attend wasn't pulling at her the way it had in the past. That talk with Penny, the group leader, had opened her eyes to possibilities she hadn't considered before. Perhaps she'd used those gatherings as a way to deal with the Billy effect, rather than the alcohol factor.

That was okay too. It had helped her cope in a very fundamental way. She'd still attend meetings when she felt the need. The support and comfort had proved immense.

She took off her wet jacket and hung it on the back of a chair to drip dry. There was a newsletter due later in the week which she had just started working on, and a new contract with a different government ministry she'd signed yesterday. It would require a few meetings to get the department contacts nailed down and the correct information sorted.

Her business was starting to flourish in a way she had never anticipated. Yet her days felt empty. Without Chris, she spent her time trying to focus on other things just to keep busy. She needed a social life.

She laughed to herself as she dialled Dad's number to schedule a movie night with him at his house. Some social life.

Then she phoned Molly. Her friend was still involved with newspapers, but now she worked for the local daily and received a paycheque for her efforts. She didn't have any new information on the Billy Zach case, but told Shelley she'd keep her ears open and inform her of whatever came across her desk.

When Shelley opened up her new laptop, a bunch of emails downloaded, one from Chris, sending a thrill through her. The man was like clockwork, a new message every morning. The missives were usually equal parts technical stuff about his work, and descriptions of the other guys he lived with. Then there were the comments about how much he missed her and what he wanted to do when he returned. She warmed at his words, feeling his absence in her bones.

The next message was from Russ Brewster, asking her to phone his office and make a time to come in. The police had further information on the Zach case and he needed to find out what it was. Thus he thought it was worthwhile to cooperate with them as they wanted to do an interview with her.

Her breath caught in her throat.

Chapter Thirty-Five

The next day, Shelley sat in Russ's office, trying unsuccessfully to get comfortable on a hard, straight-backed chair. She felt like she was at her first job interview or being grilled by the high school principal for some misdemeanour. But it was Russell and the two policemen Helms and Barklam that she faced, all perched on similarly uncomfortable seating.

"Let's begin," Russ said. "Gentlemen, my client has been interviewed by the police too many times to count. Let's make this one matter, because there won't be a lot more in the way of opportunities. At some point it becomes harrassment."

Detective Helms nodded and looked at Shelley. "I'd like to go over statements from the case that you've made to the police in the past."

Her eyebrows rose. "All of them? There have been dozens. Why go over them now? As far as I remember, they all say the same thing."

"Not quite," Helms remarked. "What time did you leave for work that day?"

She sighed. "My shift started at five. I would have left at four-thirty."

"Did you have a fight with Billy before you left?"

"No. No fight."

"What time did you get home?"

"My shift ended at nine. I got home around nine-twenty."

"What did you find?"

"I found Billy gone and the apartment empty."

Shelley almost stopped listening. Was that their purpose? Ask the same question so many times that she gobbled out some answer without thinking, a different answer from the last time they'd brought up the same topic?

After a while, even Russ was showing signs of impatience. He shifted on his chair and grabbed his phone to ask someone to bring them glasses of water. "I have to tell you, Helms, we don't seem to be getting anywhere, and it looks like you're wasting our time. Do you have anything further? Can you get to the point some time today?"

Unimpressed, Helms looked up then back to his notebook and flipped another page. "Did Zach do any painting in the days before he disappeared?"

Shelley's eyes suddenly focussed. "I have no idea."

"Why would you have no idea, if you lived together?"

She glared. "Because I had a job, and went to university. We didn't spend all our time together."

"Wouldn't you have noticed if he smelled like paint, or there was paint on his jacket?"

Now he was trying to trip her up. "No, I wouldn't."

Helms sat back in his chair. "Why not?"

"Because he was always drinking, so he smelled like booze. And his jacket was black. I understand the paint you're talking about was also black. I wouldn't have seen it."

Helms gave her a hard look. "Did you have a black truck?"

She snorted. "No."

"Did your father have a black truck?"

She hesitated a fraction of a second, and knew he'd noticed. "Yes."

"When did he have it?"

"I don't know. You'd have to find that out for yourself."

"We certainly will," he said, smirking at his partner. Shelley knew they'd check, probably already had. Did he think she was a mental midget?

166

"Anything else?" said Russ. "We're out of time."

"There is no time limit," Helms calmly replied. Turning to Shelley, he asked, "Did you ever drive on the Humpback Road around behind Sooke Lake?"

"I've been out there," she said. "Can't remember when. As a child, I guess."

"Did your father travel along that road?"

Her palms were sweating, and she laced her fingers together in her lap to keep them from shaking. "I have no idea," she lied.

"You don't know if he drove out there?"

"Gentlemen," Russ interjected. "You'd have to ask Mr Blake those questions. My client isn't here to give evidence on behalf of another party."

Helms shrugged. "Jerry Blake seems to be ill. We can't get in to see him. I just thought his daughter might like to help take the pressure off her father by answering for him."

He glanced at his little notebook again. "Chris Wright was a friend of yours, wasn't he?"

Chris? Why were they asking about him? "I'm not sure he was a friend. I've known him since grade six."

"Well, if he wasn't a good friend then, he's a good friend now. He had a black Ford pickup, didn't he?"

Shelley stalled, ignoring the gibe about a 'good friend now', and glanced at Russ.

Russ shrugged and shook his head.

She looked back at Helms. "I know he has a black pickup now. I don't know if he had one then. We didn't hang out together." She didn't hang out with anyone but her boyfriend, because he wouldn't allow it.

Helms shifted uncomfortably on the hard chair. "Okay, how about this?"

He picked up a bag at his feet and stuck his hand inside. "Do you recognize these?" He pulled out a fingerless glove, the type Dad always used in winter in the bush. He swore he could keep his hands warm enough to be nimble with those gloves on and still have his fingers free for the triggers on the chainsaw.

A wave of dizziness swept over her. "No comment," she said.

Chapter Thirty-Six

Chris fought to keep his temper in check as he gazed out at the vast construction site spread over a churned-up clearing. It looked like a sandy football field with metal uprights installed every twenty feet. Heat hung in a low haze over the site, and he shoved his sunglasses to the top of his head, wiping sweat off his forehead with the back of his hand.

The project was going slowly, mostly because of a lack of suitable construction materials. He'd ordered the steel months ago, but a lot of it still hadn't arrived. Last he'd heard, a delivery was currently detained on a cargo ship somewhere near the Suez Canal. But even that load wouldn't be enough to finish this project. His supervisor had decided to move ahead with whatever supplies were available rather than wait for the tempered steel and other structural components Chris had detailed in the plans.

The problem from Chris's point of view was that the alternate materials weren't as reliable. He'd explained his position several times, both to the general manager and the manager's boss, to no avail. He'd been pulled aside and told to get with the programme—quit interfering with the decisions made higher up.

He could do that, but it wasn't a comfortable position to be in. His name would be going on the plant as structural engineer. Within the industry, he'd be associated in the years to come with most things that worked well on the project and everything that went wrong.

He walked to the series of trailers lined up at the side of the site. Entering the first one, he found the big coffee pot on the stained counter half full. He poured a mug, lacing it with a bit of sugar but none of the stuff they called milk. He was unsure what it consisted of or where it came from. There were a couple of men already there, and he joined them at one of the tables.

"Hot out there," one said.

"Yeah, but it'll get worse."

They all understood. It was eleven in the morning. The heat increased steadily throughout the day until about six at night, when it began to cool as the sun lowered to the horizon. It was the humidity that kept them in a state of lethargy.

"Don't worry," Chris said. "It stays almost the same year-round. We're too close to the equator for there to be much difference in the weather from summer to winter."

The others nodded and put their cups in the sink. The trailer dipped as they walked single file down the steps.

Chris turned his mug around in his hands. This situation with Shelley was eating him up inside. With her agreement, he'd asked Russ Brewster to keep him informed of any progress made in the case of Billy Zach but hadn't heard much yet. He doubted there would be enough evidence to proceed against her father, and certainly Shelley wasn't in any danger of charges being laid.

But it wasn't just the police matter that was digging at him. He'd been with her for one night—one wonderful, powerful night. Now he was stuck here for three months. He was two weeks in, and already he was devastated by the distance between them. He couldn't concentrate. At work it was okay, because there was enough going on to keep his mind busy. He was determined to do his job and do it right.

But once work stopped for the day, he had hours to put in before he reached the oblivion of sleep. It was painful. He did his emails, and re-read everything she sent him until the words seemed etched on his brain. Then he went to the gym and did another workout, just like the last one. Anything to deal with some tension and help him sleep.

The door opened and another man came in, interrupting his stewing. Chris set his mug in the sink, nodded to the newcomer and trod down the stairs.

Back to the grind.

* * *

Shelley paced furiously across the foyer of Russ's office. "I don't understand why I can't go in there. My father needs me."

The receptionist glanced up from her work, a look of strained tolerance on her face. "Miss Blake, your father is well represented by Mr. Brewster while he talks to the police. There is nothing you can do. Please try to be patient."

Shelley stalked back in the other direction. The problem was, he wasn't talking to the police, he was being grilled by them. "Dad has asthma attacks when he's under pressure. I need to look after his physical health," she pleaded.

The receptionist sat back and gazed at her helplessly. "If he has an attack, Mr. Brewster will be able to call an ambulance." She rolled her eyes. "Can I get you a cup of coffee?"

Shelley paused, staring at the floor between her navy blue heels as she thought about it. Maybe something hot would calm her down. She glanced up and nodded. "Yes, please. Cream, no sugar."

When the woman returned with a steaming cup, Shelley had settled herself on a cushioned chair and picked up a magazine. Anything to look the part of a calm, collected client. She didn't want the receptionist to think she had anything to panic about. It was just that the police had searched the motor vehicle records and discovered Dad had a black Ford pickup some years ago, and sold it shortly after Billy died.

For their own reasons, they were relying on this information to steer their investigation into his whereabouts on the day Billy disappeared. In addition, they claimed to have a fictitious witness giving a description of a man in the parking lot approximately matching Dad's physical appearance. It was maddening. Who was this witness? Probably some ancient deaf guy who was near-sighted and suffered from night blindness.

She sipped coffee and checked her phone. Two emails from Chris. Her heart warmed at the thought, but she was too shaken to read them, and besides they were private. Maybe later when she'd calmed down.

One text from Lily, wondering where Dad had disappeared to. She immediately replied to let her sister know what was going on.

Two from the Department of Security in the Attorney General's Ministry. Where was their newsletter? Her breath caught in her throat. Had she missed a deadline?

She checked her calendar, but no, it was due tomorrow. They were just antsy about receiving their first issue. She'd get back to them as soon as she sorted things out here.

Some time later, Detective Helms and another police officer left the office, stopping at the elevator doors. Shelley rose, glancing anxiously down the hall.

The receptionist waved her back to her seat. "Please wait. I'll just check." She tapped a number on her intercom. There was a pause, then someone answered. "Miss Blake is waiting. Can she come in to join you now?" After a moment, she nodded and hung up the receiver.

"They will just be a moment, Miss Blake."

Shelley's heart dropped, then started hammering in her chest. Why wasn't she allowed to go in? Were Russ and Dad talking about something she wasn't supposed to hear? Oh, Lord. Did it mean her father was in trouble?

She thought she might be having one of Dad's asthma attacks. Somehow the breath in her lungs wouldn't go in or out. Unsteadily, she made her way down the hall to the women's washroom and hung over the sink waiting for her breakfast to come up, but nothing happened. Slowly air returned to her lungs, and her stomach stopped churning.

If Dad was in trouble, this was probably the best place for him to be. She'd concentrate on that.

Chapter Thirty-Seven

Chris checked his email for the third time. Nothing from Shelley. Up till now, she'd written every day—responding to his questions and asking some of her own. He knew she'd met the deadline for the first newsletter for the Attorney General's ministry and had received a lot of excited feedback from the staff. Things had calmed down in Transportation, and the Deputy Minister had stopped micro-managing her work.

But this was the second day with no response. He checked his internet connections, even though he knew they were working. There'd been something from Robbie and several from the Canadian Association of Professional Engineers. Dad had passed on info he'd found on work in northern British Columbia and the Yukon Territory. Nothing from Shelley.

He sent her another message, asking if everything was all right. He hoped he didn't sound like he was hounding her. He didn't want to add pressure, he just wanted to know how she was, damn it. He stomped out of the barracks into the still night.

The stars seemed so close in the black bell of sky overhead. There was weak light coming from the office complex behind, but before him all was silence and receding heat under a dark sky. What if she was in real trouble?

He went back inside, opened up his laptop again, and sent a message off to Russ. *What is going on with the police and the Blake family?*

Right away he got a response. *They found further evidence. Don't know how it will affect the case.*

What kind of evidence? Damn it, don't leave me here with no information.

The glove that was found on the scene had a weak link to Jerry Blake.

He huffed out a breath in frustration. *How weak?* This was like pulling teeth to find out what was going on.

Pretty weak, Russ replied. *I don't think they can do anything with it.*

Okay. So, all's good?

There was a pause of a few minutes while he alternately stared at the screen and hit *download* for his email. He had decided he wouldn't get any more from his friend tonight. Then another ping from the laptop.

Sorry, Russ wrote, *just had a client in. No, all is not good. There has been more DNA evidence, this time linked to Shelley.*

His hands froze over the keyboard. Shelley? She was living with the guy, why would that surprise them? *What kind of evidence?* he wrote

There was gum stuck to the jacket. Shelley's DNA all over it.

Huh. That didn't sound too bad.

Russ continued, *They've decided it indicates she was involved in moving the body. Because he wouldn't have left gum on his jacket intentionally.*

Chris hit the table with his fist so hard he thought he might have broken something. The cops were determined to pin this on her.

It was driving him crazy. He missed her with a sharp ache in his chest. And there wasn't a thing he could do about it.

* * *

Shelley's phone rang and she quickly pressed mute. Rules were strict in the library—no phones, no loud conversations. She glanced at the screen. Russ Brewster. She'd seen him or talked to him pretty well every day since he got involved in this whole debacle. Better see what it was about this time.

Leaving her briefcase on the table, she exited the stacks and made her way out the front door. Standing under the glass awning in the centre of the concrete building, she looked up at the brilliant blue of the April sky as she dialled the lawyer's number with a shaky hand. She was quickly put through to his office.

"Sorry, Shelley," Russ said. "There's been a development. I just got a call from Detective Helms. He's scheduling a session for you to come into the police station for a formal interview. You'll be under caution, so they're taking a further step in this investigation. Of course, I'll attend along with you."

He paused but she'd lost her voice.

"Are you still there?"

She nodded but couldn't get any words out.

"I think I've lost you," he said. "Try calling me back." The phone went dead.

She stood near the centre of the space, watching the library patrons walk by. They all looked like their lives were running smoothly. One fellow whistled tunelessly as he strode into the entrance. A woman held a small child's hand while he chatted to her in a high voice.

Why did her life have to be so different?

With sweaty palms, she hit redial and connected with the legal office. Yes, she could clear her schedule and come in tomorrow to prepare for the police interview. Then she would go with Russ to the downtown station.

She walked back into the library and found her place at one of the tables. Everything was as she'd left it, the books and documents she'd found on her research topic were spread out on the table top. Her jacket was still draped across the back of the chair.

Yet nothing was the same. The police were going to charge her with something, she just didn't know what or why. Maybe murder, or manslaughter, or another equally frightening charge. Her hands were tied.

That night, when she told Dad about her police interview scheduled for the following day, he had another asthma attack, worse than the last one. He didn't even argue as she and Lily called an ambulance and went with him to the hospital. She got home at two in the morning, having left him there under the doctor's care.

Chapter Thirty-Eight

The police interview was long and harrowing. Shelley had come prepared for a lot of the questions. She'd answered them many times before.

What did you find when you got home that night?

Did you have a fight with Billy before you left for work?

Do you know anyone who might have meant to do him harm?

When did you last see him alive?

That question brought her up short. She'd never seen him dead. Because of the note he left, she'd always assumed he'd run away. She'd spent the next months and years of her life half expecting him to just show up again.

Barklam and Helms took turns with the questions, applying increasing pressure until Russ asked for a break. The officers turned off the recorder and left the cramped space. Her lawyer tried to calm her down, getting a glass of water from the pitcher on the counter and setting it in front of her on the battered table. "They can only ask," he said. "You don't have to answer. You have the right to remain silent. Appearing like this, under caution, tells them you're cooperating. But you don't cooperate to the point of incriminating yourself."

When the police returned to the crowded room, they turned on the recorder again. "We have some more questions," Helms said.

Shelley almost laughed. Of course. That's what they did—ask questions until someone broke. She was afraid it would be her.

"You claim Billy left a note. What did it say?"

"Why are you asking me? The police took possession of the note when they searched the apartment. You know perfectly well what it said."

"Did you ever drive your father's black Ford pickup?"

"Yes, I drove it a few times."

"When did you last drive it?"

She huffed out a breath. "I can't possibly remember that."

"Why did you drive it, if you had a vehicle of your own?"

She sighed. "I drove it if I needed to haul something that didn't fit in my car. I drove it if my car was being fixed. Dad loaned me the truck when he was home, if I needed it. Otherwise, it was out of town. Dad took it to work with him."

Helms had a satisfied look on his face, which ignited the butterflies swirling in her stomach. What had she just confirmed that would make him that happy?

Barklam continued the questions. "Did you drive your father's truck the weekend your boyfriend disappeared?"

"I don't think so. I have no recollection of that."

"So, it's possible that you did." He gave her a flat look.

"No, I don't think it's possible. I was driving my car that weekend."

"If you can't remember whether you drove the truck, how do you remember if you were driving your car?"

She glared back at him. "Likely because I was driving my car. That would explain why I remember it." She felt like no one was making any sense here, least of all her, and she had almost given up trying.

Barklam glanced at a page in front of him. "We have found evidence that you were at the site where Billy was buried."

Real turbulence ramped up in her stomach, not just butterflies but something resembling a wasps' nest. She just looked at him.

"Don't you have anything to say about that?"

She folded her hands in her lap in the hope he wouldn't notice they were shaking. "How can I respond when I don't know what you're talking about?"

"We found a scarf. It looks like silk, has your hair wrapped in the fabric. It's been confirmed by DNA. How do you respond?"

Russ leaned forward before she could say anything. "We'd have to see the evidence before we had anything to say."

Helms frowned. "That's for Miss Blake to decide." He turned back to her.

Shelley nodded. "What Russ said. "

The cops glanced at each other. Helms snorted out a breath. "I think this interview is over. We're sending our findings to the Attorney General's office to recommend charges be laid."

"What charges?" Russ asked, placing a calming hand on her arm as her body began to vibrate.

"Haven't decided," Barklam smirked. "We'll be consulting the prosecutor on that."

Russ stood. "Send them to my office as well. I'll need to see what you have. Let's go, Miss Blake." He took Shelley's arm in a firm grip and escorted her out of the airless room into a crowded corridor. They headed for the stairs.

"No comments until we're out of here," he murmured. When they emerged onto the sidewalk, he directed her down the street. "Let's walk for a few minutes."

Half a block later, Russ stopped and turned to her. "I don't think you have to worry too much. It doesn't look like they have enough evidence to lay charges against anyone. But you never know. They may have stuff they haven't told us about. So, we need to be prepared. Off the record, Shelley, and concealed behind all kinds of privacy and confidentiality rules—did you have anything to do with the murder of Billy, or the transportation of his body?"

"No, no, never." Tears crept down her cheeks and she wiped them away with an impatient hand. "I thought he left me. He wrote a note and then disappeared. I never heard from him, never saw him. Nothing. I kept expecting him to come back."

Russ gave her a close look. "Okay," he glanced down the street, then back to her face. "What about the scarf?"

"I don't have a clue. Billy lived with me. Maybe he took it with him. How can I explain it?"

He nodded. "I don't think we have to explain it. That's a job for the cops. Let's hope they don't have anything else to add to this mess."

* * *

When Chris heard the cops were trying to lay charges against Shelley, he thought his head would explode.

What charges? he wrote.

Don't know yet, Russ replied. *Hard to tell, as the evidence we've seen is too flimsy to support anything. But they've sent it off to the prosecutor's office. We'll see where it goes from there.*

Keep me posted, he replied, then added, *KEEP ME POSTED,* just in case Russ didn't fully understand his intent.

Roger that, from Russ.

Chris shot a message off to his father to keep an eye out for any news on the Billy Zach affair, or of charges being laid in the case. Then he sent one to Robbie to keep a look out for Shelley in his ministry offices. *Could you please see how she's doing?*

He emailed Shelley again with a bit of news about his work, but mostly of his concern for her. *Please let me know*

181

what's going on. Russ says charges may be laid. If they are, I'm coming home. So, let me know right away, and I'll be there. I miss you and I need to see you. Xxx

He gritted his teeth and pressed *send*. What else could he do?

He left the barracks and marched into the project offices. "Where's the boss?" he asked. The superintendent was usually here well into the evening, making phone calls and checking the arrival of materials as the work on the project slowly progressed.

"Gone home," the doorman said. "Left about an hour ago."

"Damn." Chris stood for a moment in indecision. "How can I reach him?"

"You can't." The fellow's expression was determined. "You'll see him tomorrow, earliest."

"Right." Back in the barracks, he searched the corridor for Harvey's room.

Chapter Thirty-Nine

Shelley arrived at Victoria General Hospital a few minutes early for her newsletter interview and found a parking spot what seemed like blocks away across the vast lot. She was so frazzled she hadn't been able to decide what time to leave home. Her interview with the General Manager of the hospital had been scheduled for weeks, but her life had headed straight down a sinkhole since then. It had affected her good judgement. Better to simply arrive early.

She cooled her heels for almost an hour before the secretary escorted her into the large office on the top floor of the massive multi-winged complex. The manager gave her a warm welcome and settled them both on a couch by one of the windows, glasses of sparkling water on the table in front of them.

Shelley fumbled in her briefcase for a list of questions and took her phone out to record the session, wondering if she looked as rattled as she felt. Not a great way to leave a good first impression.

She smiled, took a deep breath, and launched into the interview. By the time they were finished, she was worn out. The General Manager seemed very nice, willing to share her resumé, and anxious to get all her credentials and experience reflected in the body of the piece. It was half story-telling, half a long litany of accomplishments.

Shelley thanked her profusely and managed to sidle out the door before any more accolades could be dug up for inclusion in the newsletter article.

She waved to the secretary and beetled down the corridor. Stopping by the elevator, she retrieved her cell phone. It had buzzed a few times during the interview. She knew there were messages waiting for her.

Dad's doctor had called, with the news he would keep Mr Blake in for another day of observation. He mentioned the session this morning with his lawyer had been taxing and it would be best to err on the side of caution.

Session with his lawyer? Shelley hit the elevator button as she pondered that. There hadn't been a session scheduled with Russ as far as she knew. She'd spent most of yesterday afternoon with him and checked in with Dad last night, but there had been no mention of a second meeting.

Another message from Robbie at the Ministry of Transport. Was she coming by the office today? He wanted a word with her.

He did? Not if she could help it, was the answer. She was wiped from yesterday and last night. She had this interview to transcribe, and the Deputy Minister at Transport would ask for her soon enough. He always did. For the moment, Robbie would have to wait.

Emerging on the fourth floor, Shelley started down the long corridor toward the west wing of the hospital. Dad would have finished his lunch by now—likely white bread and processed cheese—although she'd been pleased to see there were some healthier selections on offer the last time he'd been in.

He was dozing in bed when she arrived, his head lolling to the side, breathing tubes tucked awkwardly beneath his chin. She eased them to a more comfortable position, and took a seat by the bed. A nurse walked silently past the doorway on rubber soles. The other bed in the room was empty, the covers turned back. Dad looked pale under his tan, a deep frown drawn on his brow. He clasped the bed railing in a tight grip, even in sleep, so that his fingers appeared white from the pressure.

She rubbed her fingers gently over her father's until the grip relaxed, then took his big hand in hers and just held it. He slowly opened his eyes.

"Shelley," he rasped. "There you are, my girl. How are you?"

She gave a half laugh. "Good," she said. "Better than you."

"Huh." He rolled his head on the pillow, then back to look at her. "Did you talk to Russ?"

"You know I did. He was with me at the police station all yesterday afternoon." Was Dad starting to forget things? That would be an added challenge on top of all the other health issues he was dealing with.

He shrugged irritably. "I meant today."

"Oh, sorry." She eyed him thoughtfully. "Not today, no. I've just finished a character interview with the General Manager of the hospital. It took all morning." She leaned closer. "Don't get me wrong, she's a very capable woman." She took another careful look around the room to make sure it was still empty. "But I've never met anyone so full of herself. She spent half the time telling me all the degrees she has, what her majors were, how many committees she's served on."

Dad gave a rusty laugh as his eyes lit up. "Must have been fun."

"Yeah, lots of fun." She regarded him fondly. "What about you? When are they letting you out of this joint?"

He sobered quickly. "That's the thing, Shelley. I'm here for a while. I thought you might have talked to Russ."

"Russ?" She frowned. "What does he have to do with whether you stay in the hospital or not? That's up to your doctor."

He squinted for a moment, staring at the empty doorway behind her. "Not really. Things have changed."

Her stomach jumped in confusion. Tough enough that she was waiting to see what charges the prosecutor would decide to lay against her. But now her father had more medical issues? "I don't understand."

"I had the nurse call Russ, got him down here to talk to me," Dad said. "About time that pencil-pusher earns his keep."

She had to laugh. "He's been pretty good, Dad. And I haven't seen a bill yet. Don't know if he's going to overcharge us or not."

"Yeah, right. Anyway, Russ came in this morning. We had a heart-to-heart talk. They won't be laying charges against you."

"They won't?" She couldn't believe the feeling of weightlessness that rose in her chest, flying right up through the top of her head. "They won't?" She laughed, tears standing in her eyes. "Dad, that's good news. Such good news. I can't..." Gripping his hand, she closed her eyes and waited for the dizziness to pass. "Thank God."

His hand tightened on hers. "I've confessed to the crime."

Slowly she opened her eyes. To her surprise, he looked the same, his white hair combed back from a heavily tanned face. It was all the days working in the bush, summer and winter. The summer sun tanned his skin, the winter cold weathered it to a deep brown.

What was he talking about? "Don't joke, Dad. This hasn't been funny, none of it. I'm exhausted with the back and forth from the police. I just want Billy to leave us alone."

"He will now," he said. "It was me, Shelley. I finished him off. I don't regret it, not for a minute. When I saw what he was doing to you..." His jaw clenched as his fingers tightened painfully on her hand.

"Dad, what are you saying?"

"I killed Billy. I went over there that day, after you'd gone to work. I was heading up-island and wanted to speak to him before I left."

She froze, staring at his face. "You went over there?"

186

"Yeah. I didn't mean to hurt him. It was an accident, kind of." There was a long pause as she held her breath, wondering what he'd say next and if she'd even take it in. Her hearing seemed to have shut down, her ears blocked by some kind of loud ringing.

"I just wanted to warn him. Let him know you weren't alone, that you had family who cared about you and weren't going to let him treat you like garbage." His breathing grew more laboured and he reached for the knob to turn up the oxygen. Then he shifted in the bed, lifting himself higher against the pillows.

She waited, but he was silent. "Did you kill him, Dad?"

"Yeah, apparently."

"Apparently?" Her voice had come out as a shriek and she covered her mouth with her fingers. She lowered her voice with great effort. "What do you mean? Either you did or you didn't!" Her breathing started to sound like his, all raspy and laboured. This was a total mess. If he'd confessed, then he was headed for jail. How was that any better than if she went to trial for the same offence? Neither was okay. Why couldn't Billy just go away?

"You didn't tell the police, did you Dad? You can't tell them."

He gave her a soft sympathetic look. "Sweetheart, you don't have to worry. Look at me. They aren't going to put me in jail, are they?"

The light dawned. "Dad, is that why you confessed, so they won't charge me? I'll go to jail because I'm healthy, but you won't because you're too sick. That's the stupidest thing I've ever heard. What were you thinking? I hope Russ can keep his mouth shut…."

"Shelley, calm down. Just listen, okay?"

She threw her hands in the air. "I can't. I've been so frustrated about this whole thing for so long, I don't have any patience left. I can't listen."

There were quick footsteps in the hall and Shelley turned around as Lily walked through the door.

Chapter Forty

"Chris, calm down." Harvey pulled him aside in the hallway before they reached the manager's door. "Let me do the talking. I've got nothing to lose at this point. You'll probably want to keep your job here, at least for a while."

He led the way into the office. "Mr. Hasan, could we have a moment of your time?"

The project manager looked up from his calculator, keeping his finger on a spot halfway down a list of figures lying on the top of his desk. "What can I do for you, gentlemen?"

"Chris has a problem." They each took a seat in front of the desk, as Harvey continued. "He's got a family issue back home and needs to take some unscheduled leave to look after it."

Hasan gave Chris a long look, then pulled his laptop forward, using the mouse to manoeuvre over the screen. "Chris Wright, isn't it? Structural engineer."

Chris nodded tightly. "That's right."

Hasan frowned as he read some information. "You just returned from leave a month ago. You've got another two months before you're eligible for further time away."

Chris shrugged. "That's true. But this is more of an emergency. It concerns some police charges and I need to get home to offer what help and support I can to my family."

"Sorry, but not possible." Hasan glanced back at the list of figures. "I'm busy, gentlemen. Please see yourselves out."

Anger rose in a heavy tide up his throat, and it must have been obvious because Harvey planted a hard hand on his shoulder and gave him a shove toward the door. "Thanks for your time, Mr. Hasan," Harvey said as they exited the office.

In a fury, Chris stalked down the corridor of the office complex, heading for outside. He took the steps two at a time, then turned to Harvey who marched right behind him. "I told you he wouldn't allow it. Well, it doesn't matter, I'm just going to quit. It'll save time and hassle for everyone."

Harvey got right in his face. "You do that, you won't find another job waiting for you anywhere. You don't just quit. Not unless your mother is dying of cancer, and even then, you give some notice, or manage to wangle permission from someone in authority."

He glanced around, and pulled Chris out of the way of a couple of Arabs heading their way, robes flapping around their legs. "The next step is to talk to Hasan's boss, the prince."

* * *

Feeling sick to her stomach, Shelley got another chair for her sister. "Lily, Dad has something to tell you," she said.

By the time their father told of his confession to the lawyer, Lily's face had turned white. "I don't understand," she muttered. "It doesn't make any sense to me. Why did you say that to him?"

Dad motioned to Shelley. "Close the door, girl. We don't need the rest of these sickies to hear what we're talking about."

Shelley wobbled to the door and closed it, stumbling back to her chair. "I don't understand either." She took a seat and leaned forward. "Tell us what you told Russ, and don't leave anything out. Are you saying you killed Billy Zach?"

Dad nodded and Lily gasped, eyes wide.

"Just listen, okay?" he said. "I'd seen the bruises on your arms and face, Shelley. I had no idea what other damage he might have inflicted on you."

Her gut clenched. She'd naively thought she'd hidden most of those marks, especially from her family. She glanced down but said nothing.

"It's not your shame, Shelley."

She looked up into Dad's large dark eyes, so much like her own.

"It was his."

Lily reached for her hand and clasped it gently.

"I had decided to talk to him that night," he continued. "I knew he didn't always make sense, and that he drank a lot. But you left for work about four-thirty, so I figured he'd be relatively sober on a Sunday afternoon. That was my first mistake."

He took a shallow breath and wheezed it out. "I was on my way up island for the week anyway, just left a little earlier. Billy came out of the apartment just as I pulled to a stop in the parking lot. He looked a little erratic."

Shelley clenched her hand tighter in Lily's grip. Yes, Billy had been erratic that afternoon. There were other words to describe him—angry, abusive, enraged. He'd used a closed fist on her face just before she headed off to work because she hadn't been fast enough fetching his cigarettes. Her cheek throbbed at the memory.

"I didn't see anyone else around," Dad continued. "I thought if there was another guy outside in the parking lot, he'd act a little more subdued, but I was alone there with him. I climbed out of the truck."

Shelley shuddered. Billy would see that as a challenge. He hated to be confronted.

"I walked toward him and called his name. He said, *what do you want, old man? I'm in a hurry, so be quick.*" Dad closed his eyes a moment, as if remembering the encounter.

"I said, *I want to talk to you about my daughter.*" He opened his eyes and looked at her, determination clear in his

190

gaze. "You're my daughter, Shelley. I have the right to defend you. No one, not even Billy Zach, can take that away from me."

Shelley reached with her other hand to touch his fingers and he grabbed hold tightly.

"He kept walking till he was right up in my face. I didn't know what he had in mind but he spat at me. I reeled back, wiping it off with my sleeve. *I'm warning you, Zach*, I said. *Don't you lay another hand on her.*

"*Or what?* he said. *You should see her face right now. I just laid a hand on her.*

"I was furious." His eyes blazed with remembered fury. "I said, you can't do that. And then he hit me, square in the face. Hit my nose. The blood poured out. When he raised his fist to hit me again, I lambasted him on the jaw."

There was silence in the room. Someone opened the door and peeked inside, then closed it again. Shelley eased her fingers from her sister's grip and massaged her hand. "Was he dead?" she whispered.

He looked into her eyes then glanced away uncomfortably. "No. At least, I've never heard of someone dying from a blow to the jaw." He was silent for a moment.

"How did he die, then?" Lily's voice was thin, her expression set.

Dad shrugged and refused to meet her gaze. "He spun around from the impact and fell. I think that's when he died. He didn't get his hands up or anything, just fell. I saw him land."

He would certainly know what that looked like. He'd being felling trees in the forest throughout his working life.

"I threw him in the back of the truck and headed out of town," he continued, reciting the story like something he'd memorized. Maybe he had. It would certainly stay with him if he'd killed someone. "I unloaded him on the back road that runs through the old mine on the far side of Shawnigan." He fell silent and gazed at the window as if distracted by the view.

191

There was silence in the room. The door opened again and a young man limped in to settle himself on the other hospital bed. He turned on the television to a news channel.

Shelley watched him, thinking everything looked so ordinary around her, when nothing in her life was normal now.

Chapter Forty-One

It took two days to arrange the meeting with the owner of Asmira Engineering while Chris stewed and seethed, trying to keep his mind on work. With rising anger, he presented himself at head office in Riyadh after a lengthy bus ride. There had been more emails from Shelley, and a few from Russ. None of the information they contained was at all reassuring. Shelley was still waiting for the prosecutor to file against her, and Russ had nothing good to report, other than an opinion that the police lacked enough evidence to make any charges stick.

The Asmira headquarters was ostentatiously decorated with plush carpets, low padded seats and crimson cushions in the entry. Prince Fakhoury was waiting for him in his office. This room was only slightly less heavily adorned with cushioned armchairs of lacquered wood arranged around low tables holding decanters and small bowls. His thick wavy hair was cut short in an expensive style and his head cloth lay on a table by the door. He wore a designer suit under his long robes, the shirt carrying embroidered initials on the collar and the silk tie loosened in the heat.

Seated behind his desk, Fakhoury motioned him to an uncomfortable wooden chair facing the polished expanse. "Chris Wright," he said in a stiff British accent, adjusting his robe. "Mr. Hasan informed me you needed an appointment. Let's hear what it's about."

"Thank you for your time, Prince," Chris said, relieved to finally be here. "I'm sorry to intrude, and wouldn't do so if it wasn't an emergency. My fiancée has been the subject of some uncomfortable police interest back home." The last thing he wanted to do was let him think he was engaged to a criminal. In fact, he wasn't engaged at all, but he'd keep that fact to himself.

"She needs my support," he continued. "I've hired a lawyer, but things are very tense. I'd be grateful for the opportunity to go home and see what I can do to support her. I wouldn't be gone more than a week, two at the most."

Fakhoury pursed his lips. "This is highly unusual," he commented.

Chris nodded. He knew for a fact it wasn't unusual at all. There had been plenty of times workers from different projects he'd been involved in had gone home early, or delayed their return well after their leave had expired. Only one had been fired that Chris was aware of, a man who simply never showed up again for work.

But, like Harvey said, best to keep himself in the good graces of this company. If he wanted to move on, and he definitely planned on that, he would need their recommendation. The better part of his career so far had been conducted here in Saudi.

"I understand," he said, "and I wouldn't ask if it wasn't overwhelmingly important that I return home, even for a short time."

Prince Fakhoury laid his manicured hands on the desktop. "I see. And what does this police activity have to do with?"

That was exactly the question Chris didn't want to answer. "It has nothing to do with her," he replied. "It's a total misunderstanding. The police have got it wrong. I need to return to help straighten things out." He had the idea that kind of argument might resonate with the man because of his experience in the Arab world, and it seemed to because the prince shrugged and signed a document in front of him, handing it off.

"Here you go, one week's leave, two if necessary. Make sure you look after business while you're there, so this isn't required again."

Chris took a deep breath, only now realizing he'd been holding it. "Thank you, Prince. My project manager, Mr. Hasan, is well respected and has been very professional to deal with. This was just more than he was willing to grant on his own authority."

Fakhoury's face eased into a smile as Chris got to his feet. "You're a well-respected worker, yourself, Mr. Wright. We've been pleased to have you on our development team, and hope things work out so you can return shortly."

Chris stifled a grunt of frustration. If he was so well-respected, why didn't anyone listen when he told them there were safety issues with the new construction materials? Shouldn't they pay attention to the people they hired to advise their team? He realized his temper was very short and too close to eruption to risk comment.

He bowed in acknowledgement and left the office, departing through the elaborately decorated outer room, stepping round cushions and low stools as he headed for the door.

All he had to do now was pack his bag and get out of here.

* * *

"So how are you handling this?" Molly took a small sip of her coffee and set the mug down. She grabbed the last piece of the oat bar on the plate in front of her and popped it into her mouth They had arrived at the coffee shop in heavy rain but it had already started to let up outside. Their coats were still dripping on hooks by the door.

Shelley gave a shrug. "Not well. I'm not handling this at all well. Dad's in hospital hooked up to some breathing apparatus, and I'm having an attack of nerves every few minutes. Lily appears to be shaking in her boots, although she's tougher than she looks."

Molly gave her a curious stare. "What do your lawyers say?"

"The lawyer says we can't respond until we know what the prosecutor is going to do. We have to wait while he arranges meetings with the police and the Attorney General's department. It's the hardest thing I've ever had to face—do nothing while they organize criminal charges against us."

Molly shifted her short legs to let someone by their table in the crowded coffee shop, and glanced back at her. "Do you think your father confessed to save you from being arrested?"

"Yes, I'm positive that's what he did."

"So, is it true, what he said? Or did he manufacture it to protect you?"

"Molly, this isn't an article for your newspaper." Shelley glared at her friend. "You sound like you're doing some research before you start writing the story. You promised it was off the record."

Molly laughed, then shook her head. "I know it isn't a laughing matter. We already agreed I don't get to report it. Even though it goes against the grain to walk past a scoop like this." She grew serious. "Are you praying?"

"Praying?" Shelley gave her an assessing glance. "To God?"

"Yup. That would be Him." Molly looked amused. "Can't think of anyone else to pray to. Are you?"

She gazed into her mug at the muddy contents. "I haven't prayed much in the last few years."

"No? Probably time to start."

"Maybe. Does it help?" Shelley studied her friend's face, the high cheekbones and slanted eyes. This was one person who had always been there for her. "Has it helped you?"

"Always." Molly laughed. "How do you think you pulled everything together in your last year of university?"

Shelley sat back and frowned. "I worked my buns off, that's how."

"Hmm. And I prayed my heart out."

She stared. "You did?"

"Of course. You needed all the help you could get." Molly nodded and took another sip of coffee, draining her cup.

The noise in the shop grew louder as a group of people surged through the door. Molly gathered her things together, tucking her wallet into the tote on the chair beside her. "Let's walk for a few blocks. I could use the fresh air, and it's finally stopped raining."

Shelley grabbed her briefcase and threaded her way between the tables toward the door, stopping to take her jacket from the hook. Stepping onto the sidewalk, she nearly collided with a man barrelling past in the other direction. "Sorry." She took a hurried step back, but the man stopped and stared at her.

"Shelley Blake," he growled. "Well, how about that. I hear you're finally getting your just desserts."

"Pardon me?"

Molly stopped next to her as she studied the man's face. He was medium height, broad and weathered looking. Then she noticed the woman a step behind. "Mrs. Zach," she blurted, feeling heat rise up her throat.

"That's me," the woman said. Her appearance hadn't improved. She wore orange stretch pants with a pair of men's dress shoes, and a too-tight jacket. She gave Shelley a shrewd look over the half glasses perched on her nose. "I read in the paper they're about to lay charges for our son's murder. My guess is you're at the top of the list."

Her husband laughed loudly. "Caught at last. I can't believe it's taken those coppers this long to get the job done."

By now the heat had reached Shelley's cheeks. She was positive they were bright red. "Mr. Zach," she said, pointing a finger at his thick chest. "I suspect that if they were going to lay charges, you'd be first in line. You drove a black truck back then, as I recall."

Zach's face turned crimson, his eyes glittering with hatred. "If you know what's good for you, you'll keep your trap shut!" He grabbed his wife's arm with a rough grip and stomped off, glaring back at her over his shoulder.

When Shelley turned to her friend, Molly's eyes were wide. "Those are Billy's parents?" she squawked. "Goodness, that explains a lot. You know," she said thoughtfully, "that was an extreme reaction to your suggestion that he owned a black truck back then."

"I know." Shelley watched them disappear in the distance. "He looks a lot like my father in build, too. If there really is a witness as the police claim, their description of the guy in the parking lot would fit Mr. Zach as easily as Dad."

Molly frowned. "It would bear looking into."

She gave a weak smile. "You've found your calling, Molly. The investigative journalist is on the trail."

Chapter Forty-Two

Dad was released from hospital the next morning. Lily had gone to work, so Shelley met the van when it pulled up in front of the house. Paramedics wheeled her father up the side ramp into the kitchen and along the hall to his bedroom. They swiftly hooked up his breathing tubes and oxygen tanks. He looked smaller than before, shrunken by the medical treatments and stress of the police investigation. His breathing was steady but laboured, his skin pale.

She gazed at him anxiously. "Dad, are you tired? Do you want to just rest, or would you like to be up for a bit? I have soup, and can make a sandwich."

He closed his eyes a moment. When he opened them again, moisture had escaped down his cheeks.

"Oh, Dad." She sat on the side of the bed and took his rough hand in hers, rubbing the thick fingers. "What's going to happen? I'm so afraid."

He shook his head. "Don't worry, little one. It's all under control. Russ had a meeting scheduled with the prosecutors at the Attorney General's office this morning. We should know soon, and it won't be all bad. Russ says they can't send a sick man to jail, not for a crime of passion that happened years ago."

She patted his chest affectionately. "What do you want to do?"

He gave a sigh and tried to sit higher against the pillows on his bed. "I'd like to get in my chair, find a hockey game, and have a beer and a hamburger in that order." His expression was mischievous.

She smiled. "I see. Rebellion is setting in after too many days of hospital fare. I think I can make that happen. Mustard and relish? A slice of onion and two pickles?"

He gave a rough laugh. "You got it. Help me into that chair."

Half an hour later, Dad had finished his beer and was part-way through his burger when there was a knock at the door. Detective Helms stood on the step with an arrest warrant for Jerry Blake in his hand.

* * *

"You can't take him!" Shelley was running straight into panic mode. "He just got out of the hospital. They brought him home this morning!" She took a deep breath. "What are you thinking?" she shouted in Helms' face as he waved a couple of officers into the room.

When they began cuffing her father, she started to scream. "You can't! You can't!"

"Shelley," her father wheezed. "Shelley," he said again when he could be heard. "Calm down and call Russ. Tell that pencil-pusher to do his job."

"Oh. Right." She took a ragged breath and tugged her cell phone out of her pocket. She hit the speed dial for the legal office and the secretary answered. "Yes, Russell is in the office," she said. "He's with a client."

"This is Shelley Blake. I have to speak to him now." Shelley wasn't shouting at the woman but it was close.

"Please hold."

She walked back and forth in the kitchen, keeping an eye on the activity through the living room doorway. The men had gathered the oxygen tank and tubes, and carried Dad along with his gear out to the police van waiting at the curb. Helms walked behind, issuing orders.

Oh, God. They were taking him away and she still hadn't been able to talk to Russ. The secretary had left her on hold.

She ended the call and pushed the send button to phone the lawyer's office again. The secretary answered a second time.

"I need to speak to Russ," she said. "It's Shelley Blake. The police have just arrested my father. He has emphysema. When he has an attack, he can't breathe. Russ promised he wouldn't go to jail. He needs medical care. Please put Russ on."

"As I've said, he's with a client," the secretary repeated firmly.

"I need to speak with him now!" Her jaw was so tight she could hardly spit the words out.

"Please hold," the secretary said again.

Shelley paced across the living room floor, alone in the empty house. She began to pray.

* * *

Chris was on the first plane out of Jeddah, headed for Frankfurt. Harvey had booked it for him while he packed his clothes and finished handing off the project to another engineer.

He'd managed to catch the flight by the skin of his teeth, thankful he wasn't checking any luggage because they would have refused to let him board. He had coffee and a sandwich, then hunkered down for the five and a half hour flight. Stuffing his jacket behind his head, he leaned against the window and tried to doze.

When that didn't work, he realized he was too wired to relax. Turning his screen on, he watched an old television show from years ago until he couldn't keep his eyes open any more. Then he slept.

They landed in Frankfurt in the middle of a heavy downpour. "April showers," the pilot said in heavily accented English. Didn't look like a shower to him. He shuffled off with the other passengers, his backpack under one arm, and promptly stopped at the first service counter he came across.

"I'm heading to Vancouver, Canada," he said. He never said Victoria—everyone looked at him blankly, not having a clue where that might be. "It's an emergency, and I don't have a booking. Can you help me?" The first agent sent him on to another one down the hall, who willingly pulled up some optional flights.

"There's one here, Frankfurt-New York," he offered. "Not sure if that's helpful."

"No," Chris said. "I've tried that route. The best one is to Montreal then Vancouver, or Seattle. Do you have anything like that?"

The fellow shook his head. "I'd try Air Canada or Lufthansa. You'll find them just down the hall."

Chris kept walking, finally locating a Lufthansa Airlines desk. They booked him in the last available seat on the next flight to Ottawa, which was leaving in two hours. "Thank you," he said. "Thank you very much." The woman smiled and waved the next passenger forward.

Chris located the nearest food boutique and ordered something to eat. Now, how fast could he get out of Ottawa? Perhaps a midnight trip on West Jet to Vancouver. He'd see what was available when he got there.

He checked his emails, found one from Shelley and immediately read that first,

Dad arrested today. He's still in jail.

Holy shit. His heart started hammering in his chest. They'd arrested Jerry Blake? It wasn't as if he could run and evade capture by the cops. He'd just spent another few days in hospital. What were they thinking?

He shot off an email to Russ, but didn't expect an answer. He'd likely be running around trying to do damage control.

And why hadn't he struck a deal with the AG like he was supposed to before this blew up in his face?

Maybe Russ wasn't as competent as he'd been given to believe. Chris might have steered Shelley down the wrong road. Something clamped tight in his gut. Was he going to get there in time to help or was it already too late?

Chapter Forty-Three

Shelley sat in Russ's office, listening as he railed at the prosecutor over the phone. "We had a deal," he shouted. "I have no evidence to give you if you can't keep to your commitments."

There was a pause while he listened.

"I don't care. Get the police under control. That man doesn't deserve to be sitting in a cell, and he's too ill to be there."

He paused for a moment, then rose from his chair, his face red. "I don't know or care what you have to do to sort this out! If I have to go directly to the Attorney General, I will. It'll look very bad on your department."

He listened and nodded. "I understand. I expect a call from you within the hour or I'll go up the ladder. That's no threat. I've been there before and it works wonders. For me, not for you. Get the police in line." He slammed the phone down, and threw himself back in his chair, staring into space.

Shelley looked anxiously at his thunderous expression. "Can they reverse this?"

He focussed on her. "Of course, they can. The question is whether they have the will to do it."

She shuddered. "Does the Attorney General's office get to tell the police what they can do?"

His eyes took on a fierce gleam of humour. "No, but if the Assistant AG calls the Police Commissioner, heads will roll. That's what I'm counting on."

Shelley glanced at her hands. "So why did the police jump the gun and arrest Dad?"

His look was sympathetic. "I don't know, but I mean to find out. Had to be personal, that's all I can figure. There was a deal. We would turn over a recording of Jerry Blake's confession, the police would lay the appropriate charges— manslaughter, illegally concealing a body—we'd appear in court to enter a guilty plea and confirm the sentence. One year less a day, house arrest. They all realize his health is poor. They can't send him to the clink, Shelley. Don't lose hope." He frowned at the top of his desk. "This is the strangest case I've had in a long time."

Sighing, he reached for the handset. "What's the number for the Assistant Attorney General?" he barked into the phone.

* * *

She was unlocking her front door when Lily showed up outside the fence. Shelley waved and gave her a weak smile. "Come in, I just got home myself. I'll make tea."

Lily flipped the latch on the gate and walked through. "Wow. What happened to your gate? It opens."

She laughed. "Chris fixed it."

Her sister grinned. "Did he? I wonder what else he fixed."

Her cheeks got hot. "Don't be silly," she said. "Let Max out, would you?"

Max wandered in the yard as Lily took a seat at the table. "What did Russ say? You texted me he was working on getting Dad released." Her face was white. "Doesn't that sound awful? *Dad is in jail, Dad is about to be released.*" She swiped an impatient hand across her cheek to catch the tears.

Shelley leaned to give her a hug, then fetched the kettle and filled it with water, setting it on a burner. "Russ said don't despair. He seems confident he can get him out relatively quickly. He'd made a deal with the prosecutor's office of the Attorney General and this wasn't part of the arrangement. Something went wrong on the police end."

"Yeah, that's what I wondered." Lily drummed her fingers on the table. "Detective Helms seems determined to pin this on either you or Dad, whatever he can finagle, and get one of you the longest sentence possible."

Shelley set two cups on the table and turned back to add tea to the pot. She sat down across from her sister as they exchanged a fearful glance. "I don't know if it's Helms. I just know they jumped the gun, and Russ is trying to fix it. He sounded like he knows what he's doing."

"Let's hope so." Lily looked desolate.

Shelley's phone dinged, and she fished it out of the side pocket of her briefcase. "Got a text." She clicked to the message. Her face flushed, and she glanced sideways at her sister. "It's Chris," she said.

"Oh." Lily stared at the device. "I thought only email worked over there. Something about problems with texting, you said."

"Yeah, he's not over there anymore. He says he's made it to Ottawa, and just boarding for Vancouver on his way home." She gave a silly grin as pleasure flooded her belly. "He should get in late tonight."

"Holy." Her sister stared at her, then laughed. "He's worried about you." She sobered quickly. "That's really nice, Shelley. He's coming home early to see what he can do to help, I'll bet. Given the condition of your sliding glass door, he likes to fix things." She waved at the opening.

"Yeah." Tears gathered in Shelley's eyes and she turned away to hide her emotion. She wouldn't be so alone if he was here with her. Her heart fluttered in excitement even as she worried about Dad being locked up and trying to deal with his erratic breathing problems.

She took a sip of tea and set her cup on the table. "What about your PI?" she asked. "Do you hear from him?"

Lily nodded, a secret smile on her lips. "Anything new on the case, and I'm the first to learn about it. We have a date Friday night."

"A date? That's a switch. You weren't interested, as I recall." She gave Lily a puzzled look. "Have things changed?"

"Maybe." Lily gazed into her tea cup, then took another swallow. "I'm thinking about it. I never said I wasn't interested, just hesitant to get involved."

That sounded so familiar. Shelley's phone rang and she glanced at the screen. "Sorry, this is Molly. I should take it." She clicked the phone on and pressed it to her ear. "Is this the investigative journalist to whom I am speaking?"

There was a laugh at the other end. "As a matter of fact, it is. Listen, Shelley, I have something to report."

"Okay. My sister's here, too," she said.

"That's good news. Say hi to Lily, she'll be interested in this as well. The thing is, according to the provincial Motor Vehicle records, Mrs. Mary Zach owned a black Ford F150 pickup. It was pretty old, and get this—they got rid of it a few days after Billy disappeared."

Shelley's breath caught in her throat and she pressed the speaker button. "Say that again, Molly. Lily needs to hear."

As her friend repeated her news, Shelley thought back to the day the Zachs showed up at her door looking for their son. They took most of his clothes and things, but they also made off with Billy's Jeep.

Was it because they didn't have a vehicle of their own anymore or because they needed to get rid of the truck for some reason?

Chapter Forty-Four

Just after midnight, the plane's wheels touched down in a bumpy landing on the Victoria runway, and Chris was the first on his feet inside the cabin. He couldn't wait to get his boots on solid ground. He'd been travelling for more than twenty-four hours counting all the stopovers as he negotiated a standby status on some flight or other.

He walked off the plane to a stormy night of whipping winds and dense clouds overhead. Dad was waiting for him just inside the door of the terminal. He waved and Chris started toward him, carrying his pack in hand.

He gave his father a one-armed hug. "Thanks for coming. I wasn't sure what time I'd get here until we landed in Vancouver and I booked the Victoria flight."

"Any time, son." Dad's voice was gruff. "I'm glad you made it back. This thing with Shelley Blake is really unsettling. There have been a few pieces in the newspaper about it. I've kept them for you so you'll know what people are saying. It even looked like they were going to charge her with the crime at one point."

Chris had known that, but hearing it again hit him square in the gut. There was no way Shelley had anything to do with Billy's demise.

Dad shook his head and led the way to the parking lot. "Her father's in custody as we speak, but I know he's not well. Don't know what's going to happen." He unlocked the truck doors.

Chris climbed into the passenger seat and fastened his seatbelt. "I heard about that from Shelley. I'd already decided to come home, but it certainly added some impetus to the decision." His smile was wry.

"Hard to know what really happened," Dad said. "With the intervening years, how are the police possibly going to prove who did what?"

Chris glanced at his father. "Just for the record, I had nothing to do with Billy's death, Dad. I may have thought of doing something to him, but it never happened. The police have already looked at me, given the black pickup. I bought it just before Zach disappeared."

"I know." Dad nodded. "Don't worry. Given your attraction to the girl from the get-go, the idea had occurred to me. That isn't your style, son."

Chris let that sink in. As the truck pulled onto the highway, he said, "The thing is, I don't think it's Jerry Blake's style either. He's a little rough around the edges, spent his working life in the bush. Worked in logging camps up and down the island. But he's not a violent man. He doesn't suffer fools gladly, but he isn't vicious. I think the police still have it wrong."

He shifted tiredly on the seat and leaned back against the head rest. "Man, I could sleep for a week," he said. "I promised Shelley I'd get over to see her tomorrow morning." He glanced at the clock on the dashboard. "This morning, I guess it is now. At least I'll get a few hours' rest before then."

He was chomping at the bit to see her, but she'd be asleep now, and he was bone tired. Best to take a break while he could.

* * *

Shelley rose to put Max outside, then crawled back into bed. She wondered what the day would hold. She had one

209

newsletter due for release early tomorrow morning. Hopefully Russ would get Dad released from the holding cell. And Chris was supposed to arrive in the wee hours. There was a jumble of emotion roiling in her stomach. Having accomplished so much in her business—five newsletters now, with two more ministries asking questions and showing real interest, was a huge step forward.

But that seemed to mean very little when Dad languished in a jail cell and Chris was suddenly back in town. One event tore at her heart, and the other mended it in some mysterious way.

There was a quiet knock on her door, and she sat bolt upright. Who would that be? Max hadn't barked. She glanced at her radio. Six o'clock. Lily never came around this early and Karim slept in if he could. It could only be Chris. Leaping from the bed, she raced to the bathroom as another knock sounded.

"Just a minute," she called. She wrapped her housecoat around her and emerged into the hall, peeking around the corner at the glass door.

Chris stood there in the early morning light, looking broad and bulky in the misty air, Max glued to his side. One hand rested on the dog's head as he stared intently through the glass into her kitchen.

She flicked the light switch and his head turned toward her, a tender smile blooming on his face. She walked forward on bare feet and unlocked the door, sliding it open.

"Hi, sweetheart," he said. Stepping inside, he toed his boots off, the laces loose. "Did I wake you? I wasn't sure what your schedule was like today and didn't want to miss you if you were going out."

She stepped forward into his arms. He held her tightly against him, swaying on those big feet. Max tried to shove his snout between them but had to be content to lean on her leg and sniff at Chris's socks. The feeling was delicious, the heat of his strong body and the caring in his big hands. She sighed and soaked him in.

When she looked up, he laid his mouth over hers and a shock went through her whole system. His lips were hot, his tongue probing the depths of her mouth. By the time he lifted his head, she was panting against his chest.

"Chris." She pulled back. He looked tired, stress lines bracketed his mouth. That's probably how she appeared as well. "How did you manage to get permission to leave work early?"

He tugged her toward the sofa. "They have to make allowances," he said with a shrug. "When people are away from home so much, things happen. I've got two weeks, so I'm hoping everything will calm down before I have to head back."

He glanced at her housecoat, giving a small tug on the belt. "You're all warm and soft from your bed." His eyes gleamed as his lips curled in a smile. "It must be pretty cosy in there."

She smiled. Yes, it was cosy, and she couldn't wait to invite him into her bedroom.

He sat on the cushions of the couch and shifted her onto his knee. "First things first. Tell me everything. What's happened in the last few days?"

Her stomach quaked. "Dad is still in jail."

"Okay. How long is that now?"

"Today will be the second day. Russ is working hard to get him out."

He nodded, watching her mouth. "He'd better. I'd like to know how he ended up in there in the first place if Russ was doing his job properly."

Shelley looked at him fearfully. "Dad confessed to killing Billy."

He stroked a finger down her cheek. "I know, sweetheart, but he didn't confess to the police. Do you believe him? Because I'm having trouble with that idea."

"Oh, Chris." She hugged him, laying her head on his shoulder. "I didn't have confidence in it at first. But now I don't know. Russ made a deal on sentencing. That's in limbo while he sorts out the whole jail thing. There wasn't supposed to be any prison time, even with the guilty plea, given his poor health."

"Don't get me wrong, Shelley." Chris's bright blue eyes stared into hers. "I can imagine a man might do something pretty drastic to protect his daughter. It's just that there are a lot of things you can do without actually killing the guy. And your father doesn't strike me as thoughtless or violent."

She sighed and he hauled her closer, pressing kisses to the side of her head. She was such a mess. Thoughts tumbled in her mind. "There's something else," she murmured. "My friend Molly found out Billy's parents owned a black Ford pickup. They got rid of it a few days after Billy disappeared."

He stilled, then used his fingers to raise her face to his. "Have you told Russ?"

"Not yet. There's been so much going on…"

"Yeah." He smoothed the hair back from her face. "I can imagine. What do you have on today?"

"I have a newsletter that has to be finished this afternoon for release tomorrow morning."

"Huh." He kissed her again, his lips lingering on hers. His hand had manoeuvred inside her housecoat and was wrapped around her breast. His heat penetrated the thin nightgown. "We don't have much time then. We'd best get busy."

She huffed a breath of laughter against his neck as his fingers found their way beneath the hem of her nightie. At last, some comfort.

Chapter Forty-Five

That night, they gathered at the Blake family home. Dad had finally been released from jail, and he looked tired but determined as they wheeled his chair down the ramp of the handicap van onto the sidewalk. Chris grabbed the handles and helped him into the house.

Shelley hovered as he settled in the living room, checking his equipment and fetching a blanket to cover his knees. His face was flushed, his lips clamped tightly together.

"Shelley, stop fussing," he wheezed, straightening the throw on his lap. "I'm fine. And I won't be going back there."

There was a knock at the door, and Russ Brewster strode in, briefcase in hand. Lily was right behind him, her PI friend James bringing up the rear. Shelley felt like she was in a circus, with so many people milling around.

Chris waved them all to chairs and started taking orders for coffee, so she hustled into the kitchen. He followed her, putting his arms around her and pressing his face to her hair. "Relax, baby. Everything's under control."

She stifled a laugh against his shoulder. "Not exactly under control."

She felt his mouth curve in a smile against the side of her head. "Okay, not totally under control, but at least we're getting somewhere. Your dad is out of jail."

"Yes." Her heart lifted. Lily came in and they gathered cups and put them on a tray. She found sugar and cream, put spoons out and started to fill mugs from the coffee pot.

By the time everyone was served, Russ had pulled out a sheaf of papers and laid them on his lap. He glanced around, then cleared his throat. "Once again, there have been some unexpected developments."

A breath caught in Shelley's throat as Dad laughed. She stared at him in irritation but couldn't resist a small smile. It was so good to have him home again. Leaning, she wrapped an arm around his shoulder. "Very funny, Russ," she said.

Lily began to giggle and something eased in Shelley's stomach. Okay, they were getting back on track. As a family, they would pull together.

She looked at the lawyer. "What have you got?"

He pursed his lips. "It's not so much what I have, as what James found."

All eyes turned to the tall lean PI. He glanced down at a small notebook in his hand. "I've been following up on what Lily told me about Molly's findings on the Zach truck. Several people involved in this have had a black truck in the last few years. Mr. Blake, you sold yours about four months after Billy died. That was one key to the police interest in you. The problem is, yours wasn't a Ford and you kept it for months after Zach disappeared. Now, the police have since been looking into whether other vehicle manufacturers used the same paint, and the answer is yes, some did."

He glanced at Chris. "Mr. Wright, you bought yours just before Billy died, and still have it. That truck is a Ford which interested the police, as you know. The forensic information they took from your vehicle led nowhere, and they've dropped that line of investigation."

He looked at Russ. "The Zachs had a black Ford pickup and sold it two days after Billy disappeared."

Shelley already knew most of this. She glanced at Lily, who was watching James with a gleam in her eyes. Had Lily fallen for the fellow? He'd certainly gone out of his way to get her attention.

"The thing is," James continued, "I've traced the purchasers of the Zach truck. They still have it. It was pretty old when they bought it and it hasn't seen much use in the interim. My company is having forensic research done on the body of the vehicle itself. We'll know in a couple of days if there's anything there. The chances are slim because of the time factor, but it is still a possibility."

Shelley felt a small frisson of hope spark in her breast. She turned toward the lawyer. "If there isn't anything of interest on the Zach truck, will Dad still be the main focus of this investigation?

Russ gave her a sympathetic look. "I can't see it, myself. The police just don't have enough evidence to make any charges stick." He glanced at her father. "Your statement has been destroyed by the way. If we decide to go that route now, you'll have to give a new one."

Shelley looked between Russ and her father. "I ran into Mr. Zach the other day. I'd kind of forgotten what he looked like, but seeing him again reminded me. He's similar in build to Dad. If there really is a witness, as the police keep claiming, they could just as easily be describing Billy's father as Dad. Is it possible the police have decided to look no further than Jerry Blake?"

Russ made a note and nodded to her. "Let me have a look into that, Shelley. They may have decided that Jerry had the strongest motive so they're trying to make the facts support their initial assumptions."

"What about the note Billy left?" she asked. "The police still have it. Was it even Billy's handwriting?"

Russ made another note on his paper.

James turned a page on his notebook and looked up as everyone turned to him again. "There's more," he said. "There were some things found at the scene along with the body. There was a fingerless glove. They're used by a lot of people. Nothing of real interest found on the glove. There was gum found on the jacket." He glanced at Shelley. "They think it was yours, Shelley, but that doesn't mean anything with regard to his death. Same for the silk scarf. You lived together, so having these items with him can easily be explained. They didn't lead anywhere, so that line of investigation has been abandoned. We're left waiting for any information on the Zach vehicle."

Shelley felt a lurch in her stomach. What did this mean? Was Dad innocent? If so, she'd clobber him! Rage roared through her chest as she glared in his direction. He turned his head as if he'd heard her inner thoughts, and gave her a bland stare.

Russ must have been thinking the same thing. He leaned forward. "If evidence is found on this truck that implicates someone else, Jerry, you're going to have to rescind your statement of confession, even though it's already been destroyed. The prosecutor doesn't like stuff like that. There are possible charges—such as obstruction of justice, giving false evidence."

Dad grinned, even as his hand wobbled with the coffee cup clenched in his fist. "But that's only if you'd given them my statement as evidence, right, Russ? And we haven't given it to them because they backed out of the deal we made."

Russ grunted. "They didn't actually back out. The police pre-empted them."

"Either way, they're out to lunch until we see what shows up on this other truck." He set his mug down unsteadily. "I think I have to go to bed. Shelley, can you give me a hand?"

By now her rage had receded to be quickly replaced by a sore spot in her breast. If Dad had lied about this, it was the bravest thing he could have done. All to protect his daughter from a man she should have known better than to get involved with in the first place.

But she hadn't known better. She'd been too young to figure it out.

Placing her hands on the handles of his wheelchair, she headed down the hall to Dad's bedroom. As she went, she prayed, this time in gratitude that her father was finally home.

Chapter Forty-Six

Shelley sat in the warm shade by her door, a sheaf of papers in her hand. This was the first newsletter for the Hospital Board, and she didn't want any mistakes to appear anywhere in the document. Chris had stayed with her last night. She shivered at the memory and gave herself a tiny hug. It was very rewarding to have a relationship with someone who cared about her the way he did. He also cared *for* her, doing shopping, fixing things. He'd already left for some kind of business appointment downtown.

The door to the upstairs slammed shut.

"Karim, is that you?" It was eight o'clock in the morning, the usual time this teenager left for school.

There were loud footsteps down the stairs and along the sidewalk, then the young man peeked over the top of her gate. "Sure, what's up?" he called.

Shelley smiled. He was a very cute kid—long and lean, his dark curly hair worn low over his brow. "I wondered how it's going with your Dad?"

He paused. "Oh, that." He flicked the latch and walked into her yard, banging the gate closed behind him. He stopped and flopped down beside her in the matching Adirondack chair.

"Well?" she prompted. "How did you handle it?"

Karim gave an elaborate shrug. "I told Dad the truth, that Mum figured someone else was my father."

She stared at him as her mouth opened in an O of surprise. "Good for you," she said when she caught her breath. "That was very brave. I'm proud of you, Karim."

His face flushed dark red as he grinned at her.

She pursed her lips consideringly. "How did he take it?"

"Well, that's the thing. He's really good to me, you know?" He gave her a wondering look. "And I figured I know him well enough that I don't have to worry that he'll dump me or something. And if he does dump me, then he's not the man I think he is."

Her gaze softened. "It was still very brave. Did he say anything?"

"Yeah." He paused and gulped an unsteady breath. "He said I'm his son, no matter what." Moisture gathered in his eyes and he blinked rapidly as he continued, "That made me feel better. He wasn't interested in doing any genetic tests, or DNA or something."

Shelley sighed as she patted his shoulder. "Isn't that great? I've always liked him, but now I really admire him."

They sat in silence for a moment, before she stirred. "What about the other man? Does he want to be tested? You could have two guys competing for your attention."

Karim shrugged knowingly. "He's gone off somewhere. Don't think I'll see him again, actually. I mean, that was the first time I'd ever met him, so he can't have that much interest in me." He pushed up from the chair. "Gotta go. It's career day at school, I've got a few ideas I want to explore with the counsellors."

Shelley raised her brows. "Yeah, like what?"

"I'm thinking about communications. Sound familiar?" He gave her a saucy grin and strolled casually out the gate.

Shelley laughed and went back to proofing her newsletter.

* * *

That night Chris arrived with a bag of takeout from the best Japanese restaurant in town.

Shelley smiled. "I knew you'd bring food. I don't have much here."

He shrugged his jacket off and hung it on the back of a chair. Then he wrapped a powerful arm around her waist as he lowered his mouth to meet hers. "I like to feed you," he said softly. "I need to help you keep your strength up." Then he kissed her.

Her heart stuttered, stumbling into a slow measured beat that seemed to put her in a trance. Or maybe it was the effect of those big hands moving on her, pressing in at her waist and rising slowly to caress her breast. Her head drooped to the side and she kissed his neck just above the shirt collar. He jerked, then hauled her up against him and held her there, his breath bellowing from his chest.

"Shelley, do you mind if we eat later?" His words spilled out haltingly, as his fingers flexed on her flesh.

She laughed softly. "No, I don't mind."

"Ahhh." He let out a breath and pulled back to look down in her face. "Take me to bed, baby. I'm away so much and I need you now."

Later, Shelley lay with her head on his shoulder as his hand stroked slowly up her back. "I'm glad you're home," she whispered. "I didn't think I'd see you for months. It was hard to imagine waiting that long."

"I know." He rolled toward her and pulled her tight against his naked length. "I couldn't do it. If it wasn't this issue with the police, it would have been something else. I couldn't stay away. It's too long. I don't know if I can go back there."

She leaned to peer at his face in the dim light. "Aren't you under contract?"

He gave an irritated nod. "Yeah, I am. But it's different now that we're together. We are together, right?" He narrowed his eyes as he scrutinised her expression. "There isn't anyone else, is there?"

She giggled into his chest and the curly blond hair tickled her nose. "Anyone else?" Her voice was muffled. "There hasn't been anyone since Billy. I just couldn't…" She looked at him, despair written on her face. "I couldn't bear it. I didn't know what had happened, what had gone so wrong. It was devastating."

He pushed her hair back and hooked it behind her ear. "You didn't do anything wrong. You're wonderful, baby. It was all him, only him. Don't carry that burden any more. It isn't even yours to carry."

"I know," she murmured, looking away. "I'm working on it."

"Good girl." He was silent for a moment. "I have about nine months left on my contract in Riyadh. I'm trying to think of a way to handle that, because I won't be signing on again after my time's up. I've got a couple more interviews lined up this week for jobs here in Canada."

"Oh." She gazed at him hopefully. "You mean, you might be working from home soon?" Tears appeared and ran down her cheeks. "That means…"

"I'll be here, not halfway across the world." He cradled her cheek in his palm, his fingertips rubbing the tears away. "I'm just worried about how to handle the next nine months. I'm not going to be away from you for three months at a stretch. It doesn't work for me. Is it possible…" His jaw tightened as he gazed determinedly into her eyes. "Is it possible you could come over there?" His eyes flared as she opened her mouth to reply.

"No, just listen for a minute," he said hurriedly. "If you came with me for a month, then went home for a month, then came back. We could do it one month on, one off. I wonder about your work…"

She placed her fingers over his mouth. "What are you asking? For me to live with you?"

He paused, gauging her expression. "I'm asking you to marry me," he said, his voice strained. "And we would live together every second month until my contract is up."

"Oh." She stared in confusion as her fingers moved in circles on his chest, catching in the tawny hair.

"Shelley?" He seized her hand and held it pressed against his skin. "I know we haven't been dating very long." His breath caught in his throat and he gave a shallow cough. "But we've known each other for years. Much longer than most couples."

She smiled at that, but didn't answer, not sure what to say.

He swallowed audibly. "I love you. I've been in love with you for a long time. Even as a boy I was taken with you, at that age I just didn't know what to do about it." He watched her cautiously, his hand cradling her shoulder then sliding to her breast. He squeezed gently, rolling the nipple tenderly between his fingers. "Oh, baby. Now I'm distracted."

His mouth met hers in a searing kiss as his hands began the journey over her body.

She forgot what they'd been talking about, simply taken away by the pleasure of his embrace.

Chapter Forty-Seven

Shelley walked into the back of the church hall and looked around. The Al-Anon group was gathered off to the side around a table, with the leader seated at the end. She recognized Penny from the AA meetings that were also held here.

It was neat that she already knew someone. At least she'd feel comfortable with the people taking part in this encounter. There were more women than men—the opposite of all the AA meetings she'd attended. Maybe that was better, too. She'd learn things from these women—ways to handle her life when someone close to her had a problem with alcohol abuse.

She took a seat.

On the other hand, at the moment she didn't have anyone in her life who had such a problem. Maybe she didn't need to take part in this any longer. Time would tell. Her comfort level was getting deeper as she wrestled with issues from her past.

The meeting began with each person introducing themselves and revealing the reasons why they were there. By the time it wrapped up, she had a different view of alcohol.

She hadn't had much to contribute to the conversation. All her stories about the substance were far behind her. This was not a current problem in her life, just one she'd struggled with in the past.

As she walked out of the meeting, she felt for the first time that she might be able to leave this issue behind. She was on her way to becoming a free woman, Chris's woman.

Now if only she could be sure Dad was free as well.

* * *

Russ had phoned and Shelley was waiting at the family home for his arrival. Dad was doing better, having almost recovered from his brief incarceration in the jail cell. He'd remarked that life wasn't complete until a man had experienced some time in the clink. He'd meant it as a joke, but she hadn't been able to bring herself to laugh. She was still shaken by the whole episode.

Lily had begged off work to be here and James was walking up the steps behind the lawyer. Chris was in the kitchen making coffee. He and Lily brought a tray out as everyone settled around the living room couches.

"I thought it was easier for me to come here," Russ began, gesturing at Dad's wheelchair. "I'm finished at the office for the day, anyway."

Chris laughed. "No time like the present for billable hours."

Russ nodded with a grin. "Usually," he said. "In this case, not so much. Here's what the police have divulged today. The forensics are back from the evidence gathered on the old Zach pickup truck. They looked primarily in the truck bed, around the driver's seat and steering wheel. Blood evidence they found there was tested and came back positive as Billy Zach's.

"The father is squealing like a stuck pig, but the police are moving forward with charges against him. His defence seems to centre around the fact he hasn't had the truck for years, therefore someone else could have put that blood in the truck bed."

Shelley felt like the breath had been knocked out of her. She turned her head to look at her father, just as he dropped his coffee cup. It hit the floor with a loud crack, hot liquid splattering across the rug and up his legs.

"Ouch," he muttered, batting at his wet pants.

Shelley ran to the kitchen and returned with a tea towel. Chris grabbed it, mopping at her father's legs. "Let's just take these off," he muttered and quickly wheeled Jerry down the hall toward his room.

Shelley stood for a moment in limbo. Then she looked at the lawyer. "What does this mean for Dad? He lied, didn't he?"

Russ held her gaze a moment. "Perhaps, I haven't figured that out yet."

"I think I have," James said. His little book was in his left shirt pocket but he didn't pull it out. "The police think Zach was hit with a metal rod, something like a tire iron. But your father didn't mention anything like that. He talked about a fist. He hit Billy in the jaw and he fell. That was his story.

"I've been wondering about that. What if both men paid him a visit that night?" He looked around the room at the curious gazes of the others. "Jerry saw him first, and ended up hitting him. They exchanged punches. Billy didn't die then, but when the police were going to charge Shelley, Jerry fabricated the rest of the story. However, he never mentioned hitting Billy with anything but his fist.

"Perhaps he went off to work driving up-island. Later that same day, Mr. Zach went to see Billy. They had an argument and the father knew his son too well. He came prepared with a tire iron. Who knows? Things got out of hand. Remember, the witness talked about a later encounter. Jerry would have been gone by five -thirty or six."

Chris reappeared, pushing the wheel chair back into the room. Dad stared at James a moment. "I heard the last part. What's this about a tire iron?"

Shelley glared at him. "The police think Billy was killed with a tire iron, combined with the fall that cracked his head."

"Ahh." Dad glanced down. "Didn't think about that."

Lily reached out her hand. "What really happened, Dad? I wish you'd tell us."

His craggy face softened as he gazed at her. "Pretty much what James said. I left for work about four-thirty with the intent of paying Billy a visit. I knew you'd be off to your job at the pharmacy, Shelley. You were as reliable as clockwork. And I wanted to warn him. He needed to be shaken up a little." He glared around the room.

"What happened?" Russ asked.

"We had a bit of an altercation like I said. He punched me in the nose and I nailed him in the jaw. When I left, I figured he'd have second thoughts about how he was handling things with his girlfriend."

Russ shifted on the couch. "The witness said someone was there about seven when the altercation occurred. That must have been when his father arrived."

James nodded. "That's my take on it. One reason the police are so willing to look at someone else is Mr. Blake's story didn't have mention of a metal tool, and the forensics clearly showed the impact of a metal bar with a flat end on the side of Billy's head."

"A tire iron," Chris said as he took a seat beside Shelley. They all nodded.

Dad frowned. "How would they know what my statement said?"

Russ raised his hand. "I had to divulge the general information in order for the prosecutor to run it by the police. With a plea deal, they have to check if it's plausible to explain the crime and as a basis for charges to be laid."

Shelley was dizzy. There was so much here she hadn't been aware of, it was staggering. Was this nightmare over? She grabbed Chris's hand and squeezed as she peered at the lawyer. "Are we out of trouble now, or is there more to come?"

Chapter Forty-Eight

Shelley and Chris were married the day before he left to return to work in Saudi Arabia. It was a quickly arranged ceremony in their small neighbourhood church.

When Grams heard the wedding was happening soon, she grew animated, her eyes gleaming. She shifted excitedly in her cushioned chair in the family room of her senior's residence. Shelley smiled. Grams loved family events.

"What are you going to wear for your wedding dress?" she demanded. "Have you bought something yet?"

"Not yet, Grams. We just set the date, got the licence and met with the minister. I haven't had time to think about it." She contemplated her long list of tasks as nerves began to jitter in her stomach. Even a small wedding involved much more in the way of organizing than she'd imagined. So much to do, so little time. This was going to turn into a nightmare. Her hands shook.

"Look in the attic, Shelley," Grams said. "There are a couple of trunks up there and your mother's wedding dress is in one of them. It should be easy to find—it's ivory and wrapped in about ten layers of tissue paper. Then bring it here," she commanded. "I want to see it on you before the big day."

When she got back to the house, Shelley took Lily up the narrow stairs to the attic and rummaged around. There were boxes stacked everywhere around the perimeter of the space and in rows down the middle. She found their play toys from childhood, stuffed bears and lambs, dolls and cars. But eventually they opened a trunk, releasing the faint hint of lavender and moth balls. "Must be in here," she said, rubbing a dusty hand across her forehead.

Lily laughed. "You should see your face. Cranky and dirty."

"Ha ha," Shelley muttered. "You look pretty grungy yourself. Oohhh…" At that moment she peeled back the tissue paper and they both fell silent as the wedding dress appeared. It was beautifully made of ivory satin, with delicate lace edging the vee neckline and three-quarter length sleeves.

Lily sniffed. "It's perfect. Come downstairs and get cleaned up. I want to see it on you."

When Shelley tried it on, Lily cried. They hugged each other, then had to work like mad to get the tear stains out of the fabric. It fit her perfectly.

The next day they visited the care home and Grams waited impatiently while Shelley changed. Her eyes grew moist when her granddaughter emerged from the bathroom. "You're just as beautiful as your mother," she murmured. "Just as lovely."

* * *

Lily, her maid-of-honour, looked young and gorgeous as she walked proudly ahead of her sister down the aisle of the crowded church. Shelley wasn't surprised that Robbie was best man—Robbie who had been Chris's close friend in grade six and still filled that role.

Dad managed to walk her slowly down the aisle, two arm crutches gripped in his big rough hands. She was in tears by the time they reached the front where Chris stood nervously waiting. He looked lean and handsome in his black tuxedo, his hair freshly groomed. Her heart turned over in her chest at the sight of his eager expression, eyes pinned to hers.

Grams had been brought over earlier by handicap bus and sat in the front pew beside her son. James, Lily's PI friend seemed very pleased to be there as her date. Molly arrived with a fellow reporter that she'd been seeing for some months. Russ Brewster showed up with his wife. Chris's parents were all smiles and his father gave her such a hug. "Welcome to the family," he said. "I prayed this is how it would happen."

Shelley had barely had time to prepare for the event let alone catch her breath, but Mrs. Wright organized a meal at their house for the reception after the ceremony and everyone attended. There were speeches and much talk and laughter. She met Chris's aunts and uncles, his cousins and their children, so many people wishing them well that she was soon overwhelmed.

When it was time to leave, she cried as she embraced each one in turn, thanking them for their good wishes. She searched out Lily and crushed her with a hug before taking Chris's hand and walking out to his truck.

He took her to the Empress Hotel that night, to a room in the penthouse overlooking the Inner Harbour. It was gorgeous, with velvet-covered walls and satin drapes, the windows old and creaky. The harbour looked like a wonderland from that height. As they watched the lights glitter on the water while one of the sailboats motored toward the open sea, Shelley thought she might be in a fairy tale, it all seemed so unreal.

"I won't leave you," Chris assured her. "You know I have to go back to work but I'll never leave you. We just need a little time to get your Saudi entry visa organized and we've got our plan in place. One month over there with me, one month back home with your family."

He'd made love to her until dawn. When he left early for his flight, she already knew there was a taxi booked to take her home at noon. She luxuriated at the thought of how Chris took such care, and tried to still the butterflies in her stomach at the leap she'd taken to be with him.

And now he was gone.

Chapter Forty-Nine

Shelley stepped off the plane in Jeddah and squinted into the bright iridescent light. She walked down the ramp, fishing in her purse for sunglasses and slipped them on her nose. She held a carryon bag tightly in her grasp, presents for Chris that she didn't want to lose sight of. She glanced down and was distracted for a moment by the glint of the diamond ring on her left hand. She curled her finger reflexively, still not used to the sight of it. She worried it might slip off, even though it had been sized to fit perfectly before the wedding.

Everything had happened so fast, her head was still spinning, but now she had a Saudi Iquamma document in her possession and anything seemed to be possible.

Even though all the charges had been dropped against Dad, leaving him had been the hardest part. Meanwhile, Mr. Zach had been arrested and charged with the murder of his son. His trial was scheduled for the fall hearings.

The prosecutor had listened to Russ Brewster's suggestions and got the police to dig out the note Billy had left in the apartment. Forensic testing showed it was written in the father's hand. Russ told them the Zachs had a complicated relationship, where the son contributed some of his cash to help support the parents. When he stopped donating, the father lost patience and planned to confront him with his failure. The conversation didn't go as he'd planned.

Tears welled in Shelley's eyes and she blinked them away, determined to leave it all behind. It was an old story, sad but over. She didn't need to wrestle with the problem of Billy any longer—why did he leave her, was he travelling in Europe, had he found someone else. It was finished.

She'd done everything she could for her father—arranged weekly housekeeping for him, arranged meals to be delivered, and had a nurse coming to check on him daily. Besides, Lily was there to keep an eye on things.

She'd also organized her newsletters before she left and would conduct business via internet for the month she would be away.

Even the Ministry of Transport was sorted out. She'd paid a personal visit to the Deputy Minister to inform him she would be out of town, and any corrections for the next editions would have to be dealt with electronically. She'd expected another argument. To her surprise, she'd been met with the news that the DM had been replaced. The new man was very warm and complimentary on the work she'd done to date.

"I love it," he gushed. "It gives us great coverage, the articles are well edited, and I think it was a good decision on the part of the last guy that held this job. I haven't seen anything like it in the other ministries I've worked at." He laughed and shook her hand.

Shelley couldn't believe her luck. Her other clients were equally cooperative, even the General Manager of the hospital, and she left with a solid list of contacts in her briefcase alongside her laptop to connect with if needed while she was away.

She walked with the other passengers into the open-air terminal, nervously pulling out her passport and the Iquamma ID that Chris had arranged. It was difficult to obtain entry visas for Saudi Arabia and she'd spent the last week trying not to obsess over the stories she'd found on the internet of what happened when someone was refused entry. She prayed it wouldn't happen to her.

The man behind the counter seemed very blasé about his work, barely glancing at the documents before stamping them and handing everything back to her. With a feeling of relief, she tucked them into her purse.

Next came the luggage. She'd tried to pack light. After all, she didn't really know what clothes were going to work in this climate. Chris had emphasized cotton and wool, as it was hot during the day but got remarkably cool at night. She'd done her best, but there were still two large cases waiting with her name on them on the roundabout.

She grabbed the first one and heaved it off the belt, swinging it to the floor. Then she scanned the luggage as it rattled by until she spotted the larger matching case. As she stepped forward, a brawny arm reached past her to seize the handle. She jumped in surprise and turned her head to gaze into a pair of bright blue eyes. Her heart jumped in her chest.

"Chris!"

He grinned and set her case on the floor. Then he took her in his arms, pulling her tight and rocking her gently against his hard body.

"Thank God," he whispered. "You're finally here." He stepped back, brushing her hair behind her shoulder. "I can't kiss you, the rules are different than back home. But I sure would if I could."

She gazed at him, taking in the tanned skin of his face, the wide shoulders. "I know," she said. "I expected that. You'll just have to wait," she added primly, smiling up at him.

He laughed, throwing his head back. "I'll behave. I want to make sure we're both allowed to stay and don't get tossed out for some infringement. How was your flight? How's your family at home?"

She grew warm under his intense look. "Fine. Everyone's doing well. I think they were glad to see me go, I've been organizing them so much."

He shrugged, a hopeful look on his face. "I hope you'll organize me."

Her smile wobbled under the pressure of his gaze.

He turned and pointed to the door. "We have to catch the bus to Riyadh, then take a taxi to the compound. I've arranged for our own flat there."

"I don't care where it is," she murmured. "I just need to be here with you."

"Yeah," he said, his eyes gleaming wetly and wide mouth pressed into a firm line. "Here together. You're what I've been waiting for."

* * * * *
* * *

Note to Reader -
I would really like your help. Book reviews are the lifeblood of what I do and your review of my book would mean a lot to me. If you would take a moment or two and leave your review wherever you bought the book, that would be wonderful. If you want to send it to me, my contact information is below.
I honestly thank you.

Last but not least, if you find an error in this book, please email me. This will help me fix things that my editors and I might have overlooked and make for a better read for others.

In return, by way of showing my gratitude, I will send you a free copy of the next book with my sincere thanks.
Sylvie Grayson

You can learn more or contact Sylvie Grayson at her website-
www.sylviegrayson.com or email at
sylviegraysonauthor@gmail.com

... also from Sylvie Grayson...

Contemporary suspense, romance and attempted murder!

Be careful who you trust...

Katy Dalton worked hard to save her money. And letting her friend Bruno invest it seemed like a safe bet. But her job disappears and she needs her money back, everything Bruno has already loaned to Rome Trucking. When Katy insists he return her money, Bruno stops answering his phone and bad things start to happen.

Brett Rome is frustrated. The last thing he wants to do is leave a promising career in hockey to come home and run his ailing father's trucking company. What he discovers is not the successful business that he remembers, but one that is teetering on the very edge of bankruptcy and a young woman demanding the return of the money she invested.

With the company in chaos, Brett hires her. But danger lurks in the form of Bruno's dubious associates. What secret are they hiding and why are they willing to kill Katy? Can Brett put this broken picture back together, and is Katy part of the solution or the problem?

A thrilling roller coaster of a story... Interesting characters, family conflicts and divided loyalties make this a book that kept me up half the night. Brett Rome is a hockey player with a bright future called home when his father has a heart attack. Worse, the company is in serious financial trouble. Katy Dalton reminds me of Shelley Long on Cheers although she's brunette, not blonde. She arrives at Rome Trucking searching for money she's 'invested' through a friend

Sylvie Grayson has found her niche, you'll love this book...

Emily moves to a new town to hide her secret, but it follows her. Can Joe protect her from her past?

When Emily Drury takes a job as legal counsel for an import-export company, she does it because she needs to get away to safety.

Joe Tanner counts himself lucky. He's charmed a successful big city lawyer into heading up the legal department of his rapidly expanding business. But why would a beautiful woman who could easily make partner in a high profile law firm give it all up to come to Bonnie? As Joe realizes she has become essential to his happiness, his first reaction is to protect her. But he doesn't know the whole story.

Can Emily trust him enough to divulge her secret? And will he learn what he needs to know in time to stop the avalanche that's gaining speed as it races down the hill toward her?

I loved this book! I've found my new favorite author.
Emily is a fiercely professional woman who is on her own and determined to protect her little family. Joe is a solitary guy who often doesn't deal with problems until they are front and center. But boy does Emily wake him up and does he take notice. Add in a wildcard assistant and a few unsavory characters and I was up all night finishing the book to find out what happens.

When a police detective falls in love with his main suspect, life gets complicated.

...When a police detective falls for his main suspect, life gets complicated...

When Chloe Bowman wakes to find her husband gone, never does she imagine it will take so long to find him, or that in the midst of the search she'll discover she doesn't really know this man at all. She soon realizes she has been left alone with her young son and a time bomb on her hands. Then the earthquake throws everything into question. Lurking in the shadows is the mysterious Rainman who travels under an unknown name.

Police Detective Ross Cullen is already investigating Chloe's husband when he disappears. Although he's powerfully drawn to Chloe, Ross also knows that when one member of a family disappears, the first place to look for the suspect is among those closest to him. No one is closer than Chloe.

But the deeper Ross digs the less he knows, and the more he's attracted to the young wife as she struggles to put her life back together. Can Ross break through the Rainman's disguises to solve the case so he can be with Chloe?

This is the first time that I read a book written by Sylvie Grayson. The Lies He Told Me is an enjoyable read with several charming characters! There's a lot of twists and turns in this story, and it's also filled with mystery, suspense, and intrigue; all this with a touch of romance!
It tells the story of Chloe, her son Davey, and Police Detective Ross Cullen. Chloe discovered she never knew the man, Jeff, who she had married . . . he simply vanished from her life! That's when Ross, who is investigating her husband's disappearance, enters her life and comes to her rescue. Will he be able to help her? Will he discover the true identity of Jeff? Together they embark on a journey of discovery, of lies, and secrets. But with spending lots of time close to Chloe, sparks will flare. However, Ross never intended to fall in love with her.

SYLVIE GRAYSON

Sometimes you get a second chance...

MY BEST MISTAKE

Jenny fell for her cousin once before and got burned. Can she recover, or is this just another big mistake?

Jordie was heartbroken as a young man when he returned to town to find Jenny had married another man. Now she lives beside him, and he'll either go crazy or do what he should have done in the first place - claim her for his own.

Jenny is back and she's angry. Her husband cheated and she can't let it go, her kids won't answer her phone calls and her boss's wife hates her.

But whiles she's off travelling something happens to her boss that threatens them all, and then someone comes after her.

Who can she turn to? With her cousin living right beside her it's becoming harder to ignore the chemistry they have always shared. Can Jordie help put her life back together?

Jenny's in a mess and she's angry -- her husband has cheated, then left her and her children stranded. Now she works for a company where the owner's wife hates her, and she can't get her kids to return her phone calls. She's steaming mad and she's made too many mistakes to think of committing another.

Cousin Jordie has been in love with Jenny since they were kids growing up together. Now she lives right next door. When things start to go drastically wrong and someone seems to be out to hurt her, he's determined to be the one she turns to for help.

I found this a very intriguing story -- Jenny is a multi-layered clever woman who is trying to put her life back together after a bad divorce. Yes, she's made some mistakes, but as things progress, she's determined not to make the same ones again. She's afraid that Jordie might be one of those mistakes. Her job is to patch her life back together. Well written with lots of action and great characters. I'm looking for Grayson's next book.

In the 1930's, can a country doctor and a determined widow save the lives of these abandoned strangers?

After losing her husband to a deadly illness, Julia Butler is determined to look after her family, but this is the 1930's and times are tough for everyone. As the endless string of jobless men trudges past her farm, she does her best to hang on. Then two strangers suddenly appear at her home. They are hiding something that places her family in danger, and nothing will ever be the same.

Dr. Will Stofford has become disillusioned with women. In an effort to heal his broken heart, he leaves his brothers behind and sets up his medical practice in the Kootenays where no one knows him.

Meeting Julia throws his plans into chaos. Will can't turn his back on a challenge and he won't rest until he solves this puzzle and puts things right.

If marrying Julia is part of the solution, then so much the better.

If you like western country stories with a dash of intrigue then MOON SHINE, written by Sylvie Grayson, will be perfect for you. I really enjoyed this book! It's well written with charming characters like Julia Butler, her two children, Maggie and Jims, and Dr. Will Stofford.

MOON SHINE tells the story of Julia, a young widow with two young children living on a farm in rural Canada in the 1930's. It's set during the Depression when men had to wander the roads to find jobs to help their families. These times were rough. However, two surprise visitors are discovered hiding on her farm. Danger lurks around her farm.

I really enjoyed this book. It is well written with a strong female main character and a beautiful storyline with hardship and pain as well as love. I found it hard to put down and read it in one sitting. Looking forward to reading more of her work.

Sci-fi/ fantasy from Sylvie Grayson

The Emperor has been defeated. New countries have arisen from the ashes of the old Empire. The citizens swear they will never need to fight again after that long and painful war.

Bethlehem Farmer is helping her brother Abram run Farmer Holdings in south Khandarken after their father died in the final battles. She is looking after the dispossessed, keeping the farm productive and the talc mine working in the hills behind their land. But when Abram takes a trip with

Uncle Jade into the northern territory and disappears without a trace, she's left on her own. Suddenly things are not what they seem and no one can be trusted.

Major Dante Regiment is sent by his father, the General of Khandarken, to find out what the situation is at Farmer Holdings. What he sees shakes him to the core and fuels his grim determination to protect Bethlehem at all cost, even with his life.

Ms Grayson has created a fascinating new world with a lot of the same old problems. Sci fi and fantasy rolled into one with a sure hand and enormous imagination

I couldn't help but think a feeling of deja vu. Like I had heard this story before or like it reminded me of something. And then it hit me. It sounded similar to the fall of the Ottoman Empire after WW1. The new countries that came forth. The battles. The new rulers and emperors fighting to keep their territory. And the citizens, adjusting to the new normal.

And then I realized that this story is one of a kind. It has so many unique characteristics- personal relationships are intriguing, names are cool, the plot gets thicker with each page, and I loved the author's style. It became evident that I was addicted to reading the book. I'm going to give this a strong recommendation. It's my kind of book.

SON
OF THE
EMPEROR

Abe Farmer may survive the
Sanctuary, but he won't
escape the Emperor

THE LAST WAR
BOOK TWO

SYLVIE GRAYSON

From the mud and danger of the open road to the welcoming arms of the Sanctuary, from attacks by the dispossessed army to the storms of the open sea, Son of the Emperor takes us on a wild ride into danger and on to the dream of freedom.

The Emperor is defeated yet already unrest is growing in the north of Khandarken. After Julianne Adjudicator's father disappears, she seeks to escape the clutches of her vicious stepmother Zanata, and flees to the Sanctuary. This is the safest place for a woman in a hostile world of unrest and roving dispossessed. But when Julianne seeks asylum, it soon becomes clear all is not as it first appeared.

Then Abe Farmer arrives at the Sanctuary seeking medical help. Abe isn't interested in taking a young woman with them, as he and his injured bodyguard struggle to return to the Southern Territory. Yet when he discovers her fate if she stays, he finds he has no choice.

But the journey becomes more dangerous as they encounter the army of the New Emperor and are caught in the middle of a firefight as they flee toward the Catastrophic Ocean. Can Abe keep her safe till they reach home?

...a whole new world with the same old problems - fantasy at its best...

Really a powerful portrayal of how a society deals with massive upheaval - and at the same time a great adventure filled with action, thrills and even romance. Sylvie Grayson really knows how to tell a powerful tale. Strong plot, string characters that readers get invested in. Amazingly strong world-building. What more could one ask for? Enjoy.

When Emperor Carlton makes an offer to Cownden Lanser, can he refuse? Lanser has his own ambitions and Carlton may be offering everything he's dreamed of.

The Young Emperor has been backed into a corner. He holds a bit of land in Legitamia where he marshals his troops, but the skirmishes they've launched to expand his empire have had limited success. Now, his ambitions are aimed at overthrowing everything Khandarken has cobbled together since the Last War.

Cownden Lanser, Chief Constable of Khandarken, is a private man with a close connection to the Old Empire that he doesn't divulge to anyone. Although he's dedicated to his position, things are not what they seem in the rank and file of the police.

Selanna Nettles is a sookie, trained in Legitamia but working near her family in the Western Territory, healing the mine workers. But her life takes a startling turn when Chief Cownden Lanser hires her to attend a set of high-level meetings.

When these three meet up in Legitamia, the result is explosive. Not just for them but for the future of Khandarken. The Emperor makes Cownden an offer that might be everything he's secretly dreamed of. How can he refuse?

The Last War series is a stunning portrayal of a new world created from fire and consumed at the edges... sci fi/fantasy at its best...

Ok, this series is just getting better and better. The increasing complexity of the characters and the development of lead characters is a pleasure to read. The plot, with its twists and turns, intrigue and adventure, is a real joy. If you liked the first two books in The Last War series (and, seriously, that's the place to start before reading this book - it's worth doing) then you will love this book.

WEAPON OF TYRANTS

Can a criminal enforcer be trusted to protect a woman on the run?

THE LAST WAR
BOOK FOUR
SYLVIE GRAYSON

Fanny Master is running for her life. Can she trust a criminal enforcer to keep her safe?

The International Head Balls Games are about to begin at Deep Creek. Tension rises with Adar Silva, Khandarken, Jiran and Legitamia scheduled to take part. Damian Stuke, an enforcer for a gamer in the Western Territory, still has nightmares about being captured and tortured during the Last War. When his sister marries the Chief Constable of Khandarken, his life has to change.

Training for undercover work in Deep Creek in the midst of the Games, he encounters a fascinating woman with a small child and a hidden agenda. But as he discovers what she's hiding, his protective instincts kick into high gear.

Fanny Master's her parents are assassinated, and she runs for her life. A member of the Khandarken elite, she doesn't know who is after he, but she'll do almost anything to remain under the radar. That could include using someone else's ident and adopting their child, a child who might be from another world.

As Emperor Carlton ramps up his plans for invasion, the assassin makes a new attempt on Fanny's life. Damian is her only hope. Will he save her from her unknown enemy, or is he still working for the other side?

The Last War has been a truly excellent series so far, and Weapon of Tyrants is staying strong. Exciting, full of intrigue and adventure, wonderfully developed strong lead characters with a great supporting cast, neat world-building and excellent writing. I mean, what more can you ask for? You do need to start with book 1, but it too was excellent so you can't go wrong, and I can guarantee you'll have a ball with this one.

Find Sylvie Grayson at www.sylviegrayson.com to subscribe to her newsletter, for first chance at new books, free copies, and more.

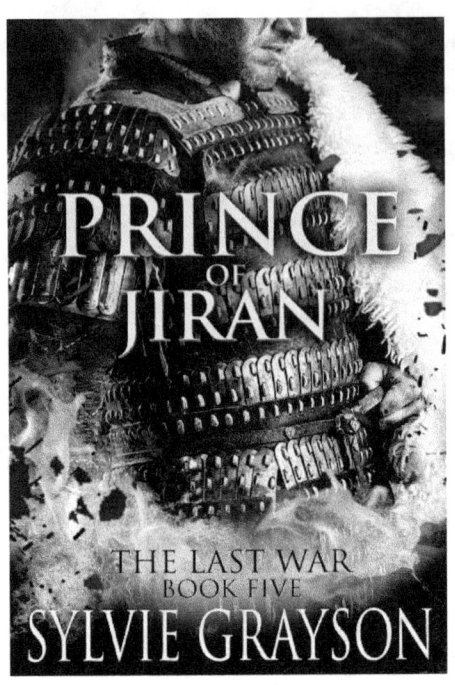

PRINCE OF JIRAN

THE LAST WAR
BOOK FIVE

SYLVIE GRAYSON

A Penrhy prince caught between duty and desire. Can he win the impending battle?

Shandro, Prince of the Penrhy tribe of Jiran, has a goal to uphold the family values in spite of his father's conniving moves as he deals with the hotbed of competing nations surrounding them.

Then he's is sent on a mission across the mountains into Khandarken to bring back Princess Chinata, a bride for Emperor Carlton's Advisor. In exchange, Jiran and the Penrhy tribe are given a peace agreement, protection against invasion by the Emperor's troops. This seems a good trade, as Carlton is hovering on their borders with his need for more land. However, not far into the journey, it becomes apparent someone is not adhering to the terms of the peace accord.

Near the tribal border, Shandro and his troops have come under direct attack from unknown forces. He digs deeper into Chinata's background to find strong ties to the New Empire. Is it too dangerous to bring Princess Chinata into Jiran? Or as her escort, does Shandro become her defender against the Emperor's troops?

Loyal Hawker has been drawn into the Banderos family feud and he must protect Angel any way he can from her brother's ruthless ambitions

BANDEROS
THE LAST WAR BOOK SIX

SYLVIE GRAYSON

Loyal Hawker has been drawn into the Banderos family feud and he must protect Angel any way he can from her brother's ruthless ambitions.

Loyal Hawker, an undercover agent for the Khandarken military, has never met anyone quite like the woman he encounters on his trip to the south. He's approached by Angel, only daughter among the many sons of Gerwal Banderos, a well-known strongman who seized much of the unclaimed territory north of Adar Silva at the end of the Last War. Angel declares her father wants to meet with him on a matter of urgency. While suspicious of her intentions as she leads him across extensive territory toward the Banderos compound, Loyal can't deny his attraction to her. With Emperor Carlton invading in an attempt to reclaim his Empire, danger hovers over the Banderos land, and the brothers show they're not as united as they first appear. During the ensuing chaos, when the compound is besieged, Loyal must work in the midst of deceit and betrayal to protect what is left of Angel's heritage. Can he survive long enough to find out who's targeting Angel and save her from her treacherous brothers?

I was hooked with the first book, Khandarken Rising, The Last War, and will continue to read each subsequent novel. The action is continuous from the beginning thru the end of each book. In addition to a fine story in a differing world, with succinct writing, there are also supernatural incidences that pop up throughout the series that add just a touch of spice. Five stars. Amazon reader

ABOUT THE AUTHOR

Sylvie Grayson has published romantic suspense novels, *Suspended Animation, Legal Obstruction, The Lies He Told Me,, My Best Mistake, Moon Shine* and *False Confession*, all about strong women who meet with dangerous odds, stories of tension and attraction.

She has also written *The Last War* series, a romantic sci/fi - fantasy set in a new world she has created. See *Khandarken Rising, Son of the Emperor, Truth and Treachery, Weapon of Tyrants* and *Prince of Jiran.* The Last War has ended but the next is about to begin. As Emperor Carlton seizes territory all around him, the newly cobbled countries try to keep him at bay and solidify their strengths.

Ms. Grayson has been an English language instructor, a nightclub manager, an auto shop bookkeeper and a lawyer. She is a wife and mother, and lives in southern British Columbia with her husband on a small piece of land near the Pacific Ocean that they call home.

You can follow her on her website – www.sylviegrayson.com, find her on Facebook, or contact her at sylviegraysonauthor@gmail.com. Go to her website to sign up for her Newsletter to keep current on new publications.